The strongest man in the world is he who stands most alone.

—*Henrik Ibsen*

I have to stand alone. Every life I touch becomes infected with Death. I want to spread my disease only to those who deserve it. I came to this town to visit a plague upon the Mafia. Let everyone else stand clear.

—*Mack Bolan*, the Executioner

THE EXECUTIONER:
California Hit

by
Don Pendleton

PINNACLE BOOKS • NEW YORK CITY

Dedication

To San Francisco.
God keep.

UNIFORM CRIME NETWORK . . . Advisory Special

Subject

Mack Bolan, known as "the Executioner" . . . also
operates under various cover names, usually of Italian
or Sicilian origin. American Caucasian, age 30, height
75 inches, weight about 200. Color of hair varies.
Eyes: ice blue; sometimes appear dead grey.

Usually affects costume of black combat garb, com-
mando style, but also known to wear various innocuous
outfits in a subtle applications of "role camouflage."

M.O.

Considers the entire world a jungle and regards himself as final judge of who shall survive and who shall
not. By conservative estimates, has slain more than
one thousand denizens of the American underworld;
considers himself "at war" with all elements of the
crime syndicate everywhere.

Combat veteran of Korea and Vietnam, highly skilled
specialist in "destruct missions" against enemy com-
mands; received nickname "the Executioner" in Vietnam by virtue of high proficiency this regard. Considered highly adept at penetration/intelligence tech-
niques; military tactician and strategist of highest
order; a master at both the "quiet kill" and the "mas-

sive kill" requirements of jungle guerilla warfare. All of foregoing constitute subject's M.O. Wages all-out warfare using all facets of the combat character. Identifies, infiltrates, and destroys "the enemy"—sometimes with wiles, sometimes in full frontal assaults. Has been known to use various personal combat weapons as well as field mortars, bazookas, demolition devices, etc.

Primary personal weapon, however, appears to remain a 9mm Beretta Brigadier equipped with silencer, worked in for precision kills at close range. Latest personal side-arm, described as "a big silver hawgleg" by official witness has been identified as a .44 calibre autoloader, "the .44 AutoMag." This latter weapon exhibits impressive accuracy at extremely long ranges and should be considered equivalent in every respect to a big-game rifle.

During latest campaign, subject was observed wearing both weapons at once.

CAUTION . . . subject is regarded as extremely quick with explosive-reaction combat instincts.

Special info

Subject is in continual "state of war" and is considered highly dangerous. All LEO urged exercise extreme caution—DO NOT ATTEMPT MAN-TO-MAN ARREST.

Subject appears to avoid police confrontation and is not known to have ever assaulted or fired upon LEO; however subject is considered desperately defensive and in constant jeopardy via various determined underworld elements. A rumored "open contract" in amount exceeding 100-thousand attracts attention of miscellaneous freelance gunmen in ever-increasing numbers. Subject is therefore under continual duress AND IS EXTREMELY DANGEROUS TO APPROACH. Various regional LEA have unofficially authorized "Extreme Precaution Apprehension"—shoot on sight, to kill.

Background info

Hometown friends, teachers, GI companions, etc., describe subject as mild-mannered, likeable, well adjusted—often even as "soft hearted." Welsh-Polish extraction, eldest of three children. Mother, father, teen-aged sister victims of violent death while subject serving Vietnam combat zone. Brother Johnny, age 15, sole survivor, escaped with severe gunshot wounds. Subject granted emergency furlough from Vietnam to bury family and arrange care minor brother. "Home front war" began during this period and subject declared AWOL, subsequently military deserter. Following victory over hometown underworld elements, subject pursued successive campaigns in Los Angeles, Palm Springs, Phoenix, Miami, DC, France, England, NYC, Chicago, Las Vegas, Puerto Rico. Most recent war zone was San Francisco, where subject crushed powerful West Coast criminal conspiracy with international implications. Unofficial police sympathy noted various quarters LEA, recommend indoctrination programs emphasizing PUBLIC MENACE aspects of subject's illegal crusade.

Rumors absolutely unfounded repeat unfounded and untrue that various federal agencies are supporting subject's private war.

ALL LEO cautions should be considered doubly emphasized.

EOM. Brognola/Justice sends.

PROLOGUE

Mack Bolan had long entertained a bone feeling about San Francisco. His ground ear had been pulling him here ever since the nightmare in New York, the steady vibrations from that underculture of the national crime network telegraphing the insistent message that here was where the blood was at.

That certain feeling was intensified as the warwagon sped across the doubledecked engineering marvel known as the San Francisco-Oakland Bay Bridge and the fabulous skyline of that great old city came into view.

Down there was a population-density surpassed only in Manhattan, and a cosmopolitan atmosphere second to nowhere. It was more than a city; San Francisco was a way of life and a state of mind, an independence of the human spirit exuberantly expressed and often wildly exaggerated. There was the largest Chinatown outside the Orient, the most cohesive Italian community on the continent, and a general mixture of peoples and cultures more productive than any similar venture on the planet Earth.

It had started as the Spanish Presidio and Mission Dolores, in about the same year that the English colonies on the other American coast were proclaiming their independence. A scant fifteen years before the historic gold rush which put California on the continental map, the pueblo of Yerba Buena was established there, under the flag of Mexico, and in 1847 it was renamed San Francisco—a California Republic community of some eight hundred souls.

The discovery of gold at Sutter's Mill in 1848 produced a sprawling tent settlement of fortune hunters which was formally incorporated as the city and county of San Francisco in 1850. From this unlikely collection of miners, sailors, merchants, profiteers and prostitutes arose the queen city of the American West, cultural and financial center of the Pacific Coast, the grand old city beside the Golden Gate which now serves a metropolitan area of more than three million people, annually moving five billion tons of cargo through her seaport and fifteen million travelers through her airspace.

Most of the city's blueblooded families would prefer to forget the wild origins of the civic phenomena, once the port of entry for thousands of Chinese coolies who were imported as virtual slaves to mine the precious minerals and build the rail networks of the booming west; the bloody Barbary Coast where the iron men from wooden ships buried their months of ocean-going loneliness in a variety of pleasures. But hundreds of thousands of World War II servicemen would forever remember that same Barbary Coast with its roaring attractions of booze, broads, and brawls.

Less than a decade later, this same cultural spawning ground had become the womb of another original American creation, the Beat Generation—and the beatniks had hardly faded from view when a successive subculture, the hippies, appeared on the scene and established their unofficial headquarters in the big bawdy city at the Gate. And just across the bay, in Berkeley, the political revolution of American youth was born, to be spilled out and amplified in shock waves reaching throughout the nation.

And there was more to San Francisco. It was the city where the toughest cops in the world had been forced to barricade themselves inside their own police stations. It was the city where the most active hotbeds of Communism outside the Iron Curtains tensely coexisted with the western U.S. seat of Capitalism; the city where students wore crash helmets into classrooms; it was the western capital of homosexuality as well as the cradle of emancipated female eroticism—and it was still a city where a cabbie's first question was never "where to?" but always "wanta get laid, buddy?"

Yeah, Bolan knew San Francisco.

It was a city of natural beauty, sure—what was it the moviemakers called it?—the most photogenic city in the world? The fabulous hills and vertical streets and spectacular bay views were a cinematographer's dream come true. But there were "underground" views of equal interest to another rapidly emerging variety of moviemaker—San Francisco was also the porno movie capital of the country.

A city of interesting paradoxes, yes—and not the least of them was its newest ingredient: Mack Bolan.

Educated to kill and trained to survive the savageries of jungle combat, this American GI had returned from war to bury his own beloved dead—the victims of another sort of savagery at home—and to declare a war to the death upon "the greater enemy."

Bolan had earned fame in Southeast Asia as *the Executioner*. As a penetration team specialist and sniper, he had been officially credited with ninety-seven kills of enemy high-rankers, and he had been described by his commanding officer as "a self-propelled combat machine, and a formidable weapon of psychological warfare."

But in that same war zone, the young soldier was also known as "Sergeant Mercy"—the GI who could not turn away from orphaned kids and stricken villagers who were victims of the brutalities of warfare.

The homicide detective who investigated Bolan's initial "homefront battle" described the sergeant as ". . . . an enigma. I don't know if I want to arrest the guy or pat him on the back. He's a killer, sure—but he's a killer with a difference."

That "difference" was the only thing that allowed Mack Bolan to tolerate himself and his new role in the world. He did not kill for personal gain, nor out of hatred or revenge. In his own view, he was simply a soldier doing his duty. His war was with the enemies of his society, enemies who had found protection from legal justice through a high degree of organization, political "clout" and financial power. By their own manipulations they had lifted themselves beyond the restrictions of the law.

In Bolan's understanding, they had also removed themselves from the protection of the law. Through their own actions and their own contempt for social justice, they had thrown themselves into the court of jungle law—and here were no judges, no juries—here was simply life and death, the survival of those fittest to survive, and here Mack Bolan was *the Executioner*. So long as he lived, those others would die. This

14

was Bolan's "difference." He was in a state of war—with those who were unfit for survival.

His jungle knew no geographical boundaries. It existed only in the hearts and actions of certain men, in the territorial environs of a criminal conspiracy known variously as the *Mafia, La Cosa Nostra,* the organization, the syndicate—or, collectively, *the mob*.

And, yes, in that exciting old city beside the Golden Gate, in that paradoxical town of human extremes, there existed a jungle of considerable dimensions.

And Death moved coolly upon the scene, and sniffed the air, and bent an ear to the ground, and knew that the time was right for *the California hit*.

The Executioner was on the scene.

And the golden city knew immediately that she had a hot war on her hands.

1: OPENERS

It was a time for war.

And Mack Bolan was not a negative warrior. His game was *blitzkrieg*—thunder and lightning, death and destruction, shock and panic and crawling fear—and once again his time for war had come.

For three nights he had held his peace and his patience, carefully reconnoitering and gathering intelligence, reading faces and comparing them with the indelible etchings of his mental mugfile, classifying them by family, function, and rank—and marking them for death.

On this third night, the tall man in night combat garb had been at his post for more than three hours in the late evening chill, quietly watching and biding his time outside the would-be swank nightclub at the edge of San Francisco's North Beach district. He was dressed all in black. From his right shoulder was suspended a "greasegun" machine pistol, riding muzzle-down at the hip. Clamped into the snap-away leather beneath his left arm was the black Beretta Brigadier—a nine millimeter autoloader with a muzzle silencer, his most trusted weapon. A number of extra clips for both weapons were carried in a web belt at his waist—also a light assortment of personal munitions, including a small fragmentation grenade and an incendiary flare. On the ground at his feet rested a flat canvas bag—a "satchel charge" of high explosives.

The place he watched occupied a chunk of high-rent ground completely isolated from the rest of the neighborhood by a couple of acres of asphalt parking area. At dead center was the joint itself, with access along a cozy little pathway winding through artificial shrubbery and plastic flowers. A man-made brook encircled the building, flowing beneath quaint foot-bridges and jogging around rustic benches emplaced in synthetic arbors.

The China Gardens, they called it, but most of it was bastard-American-Oriental with two wings of weathered stucco, painted-on dragons, and false eaves for the flat roofs. One of those wings housed a dining room, which featured a Chinese menu native only to America. The other provided a ballroom-lounge with pretty Chinese hostesses and cocktail waitresses—the only genuine Oriental touch to the entire place.

At front and center was a two-story structure that was supposed to look like a pagoda; apparently no-body had ever told the owners that a pagoda is a sacred place—a temple, not a saloon. No one seemed to mind but Bolan. Business had been good and the trade lively throughout its surveillance.

But Bolan had seen the joint in the daytime, and it had looked as seamy as most of these places are in honest sunlight. At night it was swankly glamorous and sure to catch the eye of the unwary tourists who couldn't spot a clip-joint until confronted with the bill.

The China Gardens was more than a clip-joint,

though. It was a bag-drop and a crossroads of many diverging trails in San Francisco's underworld, a favored meeting place and watering hole of the area's most secretive citizens. During the three long nights of patient stakeout, Bolan had identified several California mob captains—including a Peninsula gambling czar and the narcotics boss of Berkeley. He had also recognized a miscellany of muscle men and runners, plus a couple of black bagmen who were probably from the city's Fillmore District, the black neighborhood.

So, yeah, it seemed the perfect place to start a war.

The timing was about right. They'd closed the door an hour ago. All of the legitimate customers and employees were long gone—and everyone left in the joint now would be a valid target. There were plenty of those left.

Johnny Liano was in there. He'd made it big in Berkeley when the kids began turning on with drugs instead of politics. Pete Trazini was also present, the shylocker and numbers king of depressed Richmond who'd lately been boasting that he was getting bigger than Bank of America.

About a dozen lesser *Mafiosi* were inside, too, some of them with Liano and Trazini—hardmen; personal bodyguards who probably followed their bosses even to the bathroom.

The parking lot was deserted except for a cluster of vehicles parked near the rear entrance. The neon marquee out front was extinguished and both wings of the building were darkened; only the pagoda was showing lights, and these were all on the upper level.

Wisps of fog drifted sullenly past the lone lamp which now tried to illuminate the parking area, a dull yellow blob of light which would have been worthless even without the dense atmosphere. This part of the city was eerily quiet and almost muffled in the characteristic black-gray wetness of early-morning San Francisco, the fog and the silence blending into an entirely new dimension of time and space. The world seemed to be wrapped tightly around this tiny oasis of sight and sound, the lighted coffee house in the next block and the occasional passing vehicle along the street belonging to an entirely different reality.

But the China Gardens was the only reality Bolan needed, for the moment.

It was to be a very direct tactic, sure—but it was the only one available. Bolan had to take what he could get, pull whatever handle happened to fit his hand, walk through the doors that opened to him.

And a war needed an opener.

The Executioner moved out of his surveillance position and crossed over to the combat zone, a gliding shadow upon the night, and came into no-man's-land via the parking lot, halting slightly uprange from the darkened rear entrance to the central building and directly opposite a lighted upstairs window.

Shadowy images were playing upon that rectangle of light. The "boys" were no doubt having a business meeting—posting records and splitting profits and laying plans for the next day's cannibalistic activities.

Bolan muttered into the night, "Well, for openers. ..." and swung the satchel charge one full revolution in a softball windup, then let it go in a high, arcing pitch.

The game plan was simple ... hit and fade ... and he was back-pedalling rapidly in the follow-through when he saw her in his corner vision.

She was a real live China doll, hurrying out of the darkness from the back side of the pagoda and heading directly across his path, and apparently she had not even seen him yet.

Consciousness froze for an agonizing instant—with that shipment of high explosives poised midway between Bolan's hand and the impact point—the girl rushing blindly into the blast zone.

She was a beauty, petite but fully proportioned, the Dragon Lady in the flesh, wearing a tight Mandarin style dress with a slit to the hip.

There was time for only a flashing glimpse of her—and then Bolan was reacting instinctively, like a killer linebacker hurling himself into a busted play—whirling and lunging to grab the girl and throw her to the pavement, falling with her and shielding her body with his own. She was struggling and grunting in alarm, her breath hot on his face, when all the sounds of the night became telescoped into the smashing of that upstairs window and the closely following explosion of the satchel charge.

The entire area received instant light, flying debris and whizzing chunks of deadly glass and mortar—and Bolan had another flashing glimpse of frightened eyes as the girl ceased struggling and suddenly lay very still, her head turned to the sound and sight of hell unleashed.

Flames were whooshing through a hole in the upper wall and unseen men were shrieking in panic. Then the wall bulged out and leaned forward, and Bolan was dragging the girl into deeper safety when the whole thing collapsed, spilling bricks, timber, flaming furniture and human bodies in an avalanche onto the parking lot.

He pulled the China doll to her feet and roughly shoved her toward the darkness—and his first words to her were an urgent command. "Run!" he growled. "Run like hell!"

She ran, and Bolan went the other way, into hell, knowing that his assault plan was busted wide open now, his greasegun thrust forward and ready for the inevitable reaction from the enemy.

It came quickly. Three men staggered from the rear door and into the light of the disaster, and immediately a strangled voice cried, "Jesus Christ, it's *him!*"

The Executioner acknowledged their presence and recognition with a sweeping welcome from the machine pistol, and they all lay down quickly, brothers of the blood for real, now.

Another man ran into the scene from the front of the building. He slid to a confused halt, then began a flatfooted, backwards dance, crouching and firing at the apparition in black with a snubnosed revolver.

Bolan calmly stood his ground and zipped the guy with a short burst from the greasegun, the firetrack sweeping up from ground level, splitting the target up the middle and punching him over onto his back.

The Executioner went on, advancing across the bloodied body, and he met another pair at the corner of the building with a blazing criss-cross burst that sent them rolling along the walkway. A third man from that same group scampered back through the main entrance, evidently preferring the inferno in there to the hell outside.

And then a new and familiar element was added to the chaotic environment—a police siren was screaming up from the Fisherman's Wharf area.

Bolan checked his impulse to follow the fleeing *Mafioso* into the pagoda and instead whirled about and returned to the parking lot. He paused there long enough to press a marksman's medal into the limp hand of a fallen gunner, then he fell back along the flagstoned walkway.

A secondary explosion occurred somewhere inside the joint. A portion of the roof fell in and the flames leapt higher.

More sirens now . . . coming in from every direction . . . and Bolan mentally tipped his hat to the quick reaction by the city—but his numbers had never been more critical, and he knew that a successful retreat was becoming less likely with every step he took.

A line of automobiles had come to a halt just up-range from the disaster area and a collection of people were standing around in tight little groups and gawking at the spectacular fire.

One of the onlookers spotted the armed man in black, and he reacted visibly. Bolan stepped back and went the other way.

A police cruiser flashed across the street down range, and the deep rumbling of fire trucks had now joined the sounds of the night.

Yeah . . . he had overplayed his numbers, all right.

The enemy had regrouped outside the flaming building, and a lot of arm-waving and signal-calling was happening down there now. They would be organized into a hot pursuit, very soon now.

Sirens were flying all around the area—and Bolan had known what to expect if he dallied too long at the scene of combat. The entire neighborhood would be sealed off—by police and fire equipment—and the Executioner would be contained within a painfully small hunting preserve, with irate *Mafiosi* turning every rock in a search for their most hated enemy.

Yeah. So what the hell. It was what a guy could expect when he opened with a wild card.

But it was the China doll who'd made the difference. Except for her, he would have been free and clear before anyone had realized exactly what happened.

Bolan was poised there, at the edge of hell, his senses flaring out through the night in an intuitive search for the best road back.

And then she was there again, moving out of the darkness precisely as she had done before, except that this time she seemed to be targeting directly on the man in black and she was showing him a tiny automatic which somehow managed to look large and menacing in that petite hand.

He allowed her to gaze into the bore of the greasegun for a second before he told her, "You're not the enemy."

"Worse than that," she replied in a voice that almost smiled. "I could be a friend."

He shrugged and said, "You've got about a second to decide which."

"That's your decision," she told him. "Will you follow me?"

Bolan hesitated for only an instant—to sample the atmospheric developments about him—and it was all there, all the elements that could spell entrapment, defeat, and the end of a highly important war.

It had been a good opener, sure. But only if the war remained open.

"Why not?" he said, in response to the girl's question. "Let's go."

24

She spun about and glided gracefully back through the synthetic gardens, keeping to the shadows and moving surely along an arcing path toward the far side.

Bolan kept her in sight, his weapon at the ready, and his instincts in quivering alertness.

Whatever and whomever the China doll was, she was at least an unknown factor, a variable. It was more than Bolan could say for anything else awaiting him in that mist-shrouded night.

Sure, he'd follow her. To his grave, maybe.

But, then, all of Bolan's roads led inevitably to that same point, anyway. Maybe this one would be a bit longer, a bit more scenic, than any of the others presently available.

A guy had to follow his stars.

And somehow, for openers, this one seemed right. A China doll leading him out of a synthetic Chinese hell.

But into where?

Bolan scowled, hugged his weapon, and followed his guide into the unknown.

At least one thing was certain. He had drawn blood at San Francisco, and soon it would be flowing in buckets—his own very probably included.

For good or for bad, another Executioner war was underway.

2: WAR ZONE

Half of the firefighting equipment in the city seemed to be spotted around the China Gardens. Fire hoses were strung out in precise patterns and firemen swarmed everywhere, many of them wearing asbestos gear and equipped with oxygen masks.

It was a real scorcher. It was a damned lucky thing that this joint was sitting out by itself this way, or half of North Beach would have gone up with it.

Detective Sergeant Bill Phillips of the Brushfire Squad paced restlessly about the Life Emergency command post, trying to put the pieces together in his mind and impatiently waiting to get down onto the scene.

The Life Emergency—LE—people had found very little of life to worry about. Six victims were dead of gunshot wounds, another four had been killed instantly in the blast, and God only knew how many they'd find cremated inside—if they could ever get in there for a look-see.

Another police cruiser eased through the confusion and came to a halt inside the emergency perimeter. The heavy man in blue who descended from it was the Harbor Precinct boss, Captain Barney Gibson, a tough old cop with many ups and downs in his spotted career.

Gibson did not like black people—and Sgt. Phillips had a personal radar that detected such feelings, since Phillips himself was a black man—but he joined the Captain immediately and gave him a limp salute, not acknowledged.

They stood shoulder to shoulder in a brooding silence for a long moment, then the sergeant commented, "You've got a messy one here, Cap'n."

"Figure it's a Brushfire?" Gibson sourly inquired.

The Sergeant cocked his head and scratched absently at his neck. "Don't know," he admitted. "Right now it's just a damn mess. I happened to be in the neighborhood when the call came down ... so I dropped in. It might be a Brushfire. What do you think?"

Gibson shrugged his beefy shoulders. "This is a mob joint. Or it was."

"Yes sir. That's one reason for all the heat, I guess. Fire Department says the basement of that east wing was a regular liquor warehouse. And I'll bet every drop of it was contraband."

"How many gunshot victims?" Gibson asked, ignoring the other information.

Phillips sighed. "Six."

The Captain whistled through his teeth. "That many."

"Life Emergency says another four died in the initial blast. They think it was caused by an explosives charge."

"It figures." Gibson sniffed and swiped at his nose with the back of his hand. "Fog's bad tonight," he commented.

"It's bad every night," Phillips said.

"Who's in charge?"

"Lt. Warnicke. He's inside, looking over the victims."

Captain Gibson grunted and ambled off toward the LE van. Phillips hesitated momentarily, then followed the veteran cop into the rolling medical center.

Warnicke was at the far end, in the DOA section, drinking coffee and talking with two white-clad medics. He was a tall, graceful man with a touch of silver at his temples and a deceptively mild set to his facial features.

The Lieutenant looked up with an expectant grimace as the new arrivals joined the clutch at DOA. "Don't you ever sleep, Barney?" he greeted the Captain.

"When I can," Gibson growled. He elbowed his way forward and helped himself to the coffee as Warnicke and Phillips exchanged grim smiles, then the Harbor boss demanded, "Okay, give me the score."

Warnicke stared thoughtfully into his cup and quietly replied, "Joe Fasco, Johnny Liano, Pete Trazini—all very dead, plus seven minor—"

The Captain interrupted the report with, "I had a talk with Fasco just last week. Told him I couldn't tolerate much more of this. Told him to clean his joint up or I'd close him down."

The two junior officers exhanged glances and Warnicke said, "Well it's clean now."

"Best way to beat the mob is just leave 'em alone, I guess," Gibson went on. "I been saying that for years. Leave 'em alone, they're their own worst enemies."

A medic grinned and commented, "I was just read-

28

ing something along that line. A study of violent deaths by mobsters shows that most of them die at the hands of their own kind."

"Not any more," Lt. Warnicke said. He produced a folded cloth from his breast pocket, opened it, and placed it on the table.

Gibson leaned forward to glare at a metallic object which had been wrapped in the cloth. "What's that?" he asked.

"That," Warnicke told him, "is a military marksman's medal."

"Aw shit," the Captain said.

"One of the dead hoods is Greasy Waters. We pried that medal out of his fist."

It was an involuntary exclamation from Bill Phillips. "Mack Bolan!"

"You telling me that goddam guy is in our town now?" Gibson said angrily.

"It would appear so," Warnicke replied with a sigh.

Sgt. Phillips spun about and went rapidly out of there, making fast tracks to his cruiser.

So Mack Bolan had come to town! And, all of a sudden, the pieces had come together in the Brushfire cop's head.

The Brushfire Squad was a special police detail which had been established for quick reaction against organized violence in this age of growing political anarchy—it was, in a sense, a combat team which was fully prepared to take up the defense of any threatened civic institution—or so they hoped. So far their activities had been confined mostly to a defense of their own police stations, but they had also investigated bomb threats, arson cases, campus violence and a variety of other radical threats against the city.

And if Mack Bolan's presence in town did not constitute a bonafide. . . .

Phillips reached his cruiser and swung inside for a report to his operations center. "This is Bravo Three," he announced into the special radio net. "Possible Brushfire Alert, repeat, possible alert. I'm coming in for conference."

He returned the microphone to its bracket and put the car in motion, picking his way carefully across the disaster zone, and to himself he muttered, "Brushfire, hell. It's Little World War Three."

Capo Mafioso Roman DeMarco, at the age of seventy-two was a bit too old for early morning fireworks —and the testy lines of the usually genial face plainly showed his displeasure over getting dragged out of a warm bed at such an uncomfortable hour.

The lights were blazing on all three floors of the ancient mansion atop Russian Hill, and the place was filling up fast with the family rank and file as worried faces and angry voices continued to arrive in response to the urgent summons from *Don* DeMarco.

The *Capo's* strong right arm—enforcer Franco Laurentis—had been among the earliest arrivals. He had come complete with his usual retinue of hard-eyed, silent torpedoes who seemed to have worked out some method of communication which was restricted entirely to eye movements and facial expressions.

Underbosses Vincenzo Ciprio and Thomas Vericci were also present. They were the demigods of, respectively, the East Bay and the San Francisco Peninsula—and each had brought several lieutenants and their cadres to the big house on the hill.

A foot patrol of hardmen had been deployed along the streets surrounding the house; others cruised the neighborhood in gunmobiles or sat in solemn stake-outs at various approaches to the family home.

The Northern California arm of *La Cosa Nostra* was taking no chances with the wildass bastard in black who had moved his thunder and lightning to their sacred territories.

The *Capo*, appropriately clad for the formalities of the night in silk pajamas and a brocade robe with designs in heavy gold thread, was holding court in the library and explaining the seriousness of the situation to the ranking members.

"So this boy has no doubt come here looking for some more expensive glory," he concluded. "And I guess everybody here knows that we're all in for a damn lot of trouble. Unless we can get to this boy first and tear his head off and throw it in the bay."

Thomas Vericci, lord of the peninsular area, nervously cleared his throat to inquire, "Can we be sure this really was the guy, *Don* DeMarco? I mean, what if somebody else just wants to make it *look* that way? Just to get us off guard or something, I mean."

"Either way," DeMarco replied patiently, "it's a lot of trouble, and we don't need any of that."

A small dark man who had been almost hidden in the shadow of the *Capo* spoke up with, "I beg your pardon."

"Spit it out, Matty," the *Capo* said softly.

"Well there ain't no mistaking in my mind. I saw the guy. I saw him with these two eyes right here, and I'm telling you it was him. It was Mack Bolan. He

31

was dressed all in black like a fuckin'—excuse me, *Don* DeMarco—like a damn executioner. And the way he walked was like a fuckin'—a damn cat—you know a panther or something. I mean that was *him!* I was as close to him as I am to you right now, Mr. Vericci, and I seen them fuckin'—excuse me, them damn eyes of his, like two chunks of ice, and I guess I'm alive by a grace of God or something."

Enforcer Laurentis coldly declared, "What you mean is, you're alive because you turned your ass to him and ran away, that's what you mean, Matty."

"Yessir, I sure did, and I ain't ashamed of that. That guy had a fuckin'—a machine gun and he was cutting down everything in sight. I ran back inside to get some more help. He'd already blowed up the goddam joint and set everything on fire. I wasn't about to face down a guy like—"

"You shut up, Matty!" Laurentis snarled.

"Yessir, I beg your pardon, I was just. . . ."

"Franco is right, Matty," the *Capo* said. "You shouldn't go around spouting off your mouth like that, about how mean this Bolan is. Our boys are already nervous enough. You watch it what you say. Understand?"

"Yessir, I'm sorry."

"That Bolan is just a lucky *punk!*" Laurentis said angrily. "He's got hisself a big reputation just because of talk like that! I don't wanta hear no more of it!"

"Yessir," Matty said humbly.

The *Capo* quietly observed, "I'm happy to hear that you're not nervous about this Bolan, Franco."

"I'm not a bit nervous, *Don* DeMarco."

"That's good, because he's going to be your worry."

The enforcer's eyes roamed to the other rankholders as he replied, "I wouldn't stand for it no other way."

"Fine, then that's settled," DeMarco said, sighing. "Tommy ... Vince ... I want you both to shut everything down. I mean everything. Understand? Don't give this guy one little movement to grab onto."

Vericci stared at the glowing tip of his cigar and replied, "Even my Montgomery Street operation?"

The *Capo* nodded his head. "Even that. You don't move anything."

"I got a big deal, boss, just trembling at the finish line."

"Then let it tremble. Shut it down."

"We can't just shut down *every* thing," the East Bay boss declared in an unhappy tone. "Like my powder network. We stop supplying horse and we're going to have a town full of crazy people over there before the sun sets again. The other stuff, maybe okay. But not the horse. Some of those habits are running a hundred bills a day."

Ciprio's Berkeley lieutenant hurried in to support his boss. "That's right," he said. "Some of those heads are popping four and five caps a day. We cut 'em off cold, anything could happen. If we freeze the horse, the whole town might go up in smoke."

DeMarco drummed his fingers on the table for a moment, then he asked Ciprio, "How much dump have you been laying on your retailers?"

"Just like we agreed," the underboss replied. "We give them three days, and that's the limit. And a third of those are due for re-supply today."

"Well I don't care," the *Capo* declared stubbornly. "You got to freeze, and that's my decision."

33

"Sure, okay," Ciprio replied, his voice muffled with anger.

"Franco, that's another worry you got. You make sure nobody gets assy with me, you make sure the freeze sticks."

"It'll stick," the enforcer assured his *Capo*.

Ciprio and Vericci stared at their fingertips, their faces utter blanks.

"And get Bolan. Bring his head to me."

"I'll gift wrap it."

"I don't care how it comes, just so it gets here. I want to kick it in the bay myself. Understand? Myself."

"You will, I promise that."

"Okay." The old man got to his feet.

Vericci asked, "What about a wake for Joe and our other friends?"

"Forget that for now," the *Capo* said sadly. "We'll make it up to them later."

The boss went out and the small man, Matty, followed quickly behind him.

The others remained at the conference table, eyes downcast with unhappy thoughts.

Presently Thomas Vericci sighed and remarked, "Well, this bastard is hitting us right where it hurts. Now just how long do you suppose we've got to play dead? I got a two million dollar import deal that's going to die quick if I don't pick up on it."

"The old man panicked," Ciprio said. "He's just—"

"He's just following orders," the enforcer declared heavily. "The *commissione* has put out these guidelines, and this is the way they say to play it. So if anyone here don't like it, just go pick up that red phone and make your complaint to you-know-where."

34

"Do they know?" Ciprio asked quickly. "I mean, do they know that Bolan hit us tonight?"

"Of course they know," Laurentis told him. "That's the first thing the old man did—was notify them."

"I guess we're going to have the Taliferi swarming all over us now," a lieutenant said dismally, referring to the mob's national *gestapo*.

"I guess," Laurentis agreed. "If we don't get to Bolan quick."

"Not *we* ... *you*," Vericci said. "Remember? You wouldn't stand for it any other way."

Ciprio laughed and a couple of his lieutenants joined with him.

Coldly, Laurentis said, "You stupid shits. You stupid fucking shits."

"I don't see anything to laugh at, neither," Vericci commented. "The fact is, all of us have got to worry about this Bolan. Right, Franco?"

"Right is right," the enforcer growled. "I was putting that on for the old man's sake—that stiff upper lip stuff, I mean. We got a hell of a serious thing on our hands here, and I guess we better all face up to that right now. Look, anybody in their right minds stopped laughing at this Bolan boy a hell of a long time ago."

Vericci was nodding his head in agreement. "I saw what he did down in Palm Springs," he declared quietly.

"Right, he tore through there like a hurricane—and when he left, all anybody could say was, 'What the hell happened?' That is, anybody who was left alive. Now we got the bastard here. And you all heard Matty. He's right, you know. That guy comes on

35

strong ... *damned* strong. So we got to put it all together that's all."

"I don't see how one guy could be all that bad," a lieutenant commented.

Laurentis growled, "Well go tell it to New York, and to Chi and Vegas. Go tell it in L.A. and Palm Springs. I'm telling you, we got a hell of a thing on our hands here."

"So what is it you're saying, Franco?" Vericci asked. "What do you want us to do? Turn everything we got over to you?"

"Exactly," the enforcer replied.

The two underbosses locked eyes briefly, and some unspoken understanding moved between them.

Ciprio sighed and said, "Well, if we got a business freeze ... then I guess ... why not? The sooner you crack this guy the sooner we can get back to normal. Okay. Everything I got is yours to command, Franco."

"Me too," Vericci said quietly.

Ciprio added, "Except. ..."

"Except what?"

"Except you got just twenty-four hours. That's all."

"That's not enough," the enforcer angrily replied.

"That's all you got," Ciprio insisted. "That's all any of us has got. And then it all starts to cave in. How about those niggers over in Fillmore, Tommy? How long will it take them to realize that they're on their own? And how about the slant-eyes down on Grant? You willing to give them two or three days to get their tongs on the streets again?"

"Ah hell, I don't know," Vericci said.

"Well I do. And I got the same problems over in Richmond—also that bunch of sickle-and-hammer do-

does in Oakland. Now we just can't go and freeze ourselves out of the action for more than a day, I know that. I'll tell you all, *Don* DeMarco with you, I've worked too hard to get this territory humming the way I want it. I ain't about to lose it now to some asshole soldier boy who thinks—"

"Bullshit!" Laurentis yelled. "Can't you understand nothing? This boy don't want your damned *territories!* He wants your *blood*, man, your *blood!* You can't limit me to no twenty-four hours for a hit like this!"

Vericci calmly moved in as peacemaker. "Franco's right, Vinnie. We can't tie his hands with unrealistic conditions. What d'ya want, Franco? Just tell us what you want."

"I want every rodman, every street soldier, every runner—I want every damn bookie and pimp and whore and bagman this town has got. I want all your union boys—the bartenders and waiters and cabbies and everybody. I even want the shoeshine boys and newspaper boys, the strippers and the musicians and everything else we got a handle on or a gig into. I want a damned *army* out on those streets, in the bars and the hotels and anywheres else this guy might want to light down. And I don't want no excuses or hardship cases. I mean I don't want no sick stomachs or aching heads or falling arches or any of that crap. I want *vigilance*—I want a town that's all eyes, ears, and noses—and I want it around the clock and everywheres within running distance of here."

Ciprio said "*Whooosh.*"

"That's what it's going to take," Laurentis insisted. "I been studying this boy's footwork. I know how to bag him, but I got to have the troops, I got to have them."

"I wonder if Roman called Mr. King," Vericci mused.

"I figure he would, yeah, I think so," Laurentis replied.

"We might get some help from that direction."

"We might, yeah," the enforcer agreed. "But we can't count on it. We got to figure it's our problem and ours alone. That's the way I figure it."

"Okay, go to it," Vericci told him. "We'll put out the word, don't worry. Same telephone setup?"

Laurentis nodded. "The same."

"Okay. We'll put out a net like this town has never seen before. We'll locate him, Franco. The rest will be up to you and your boys."

"Hell, I can hardly wait," the enforcer said. He pushed himself away from the table and strode to the door.

Almost as though some sixth sense had telegraphed his movement, the library door swung open and two of the silk-suited torpedoes met the enforcer in the open doorway. They fell in behind him, already others were leading the way across the foyer, and the Bay Area storm troopers made their impressive exit without a word spoken between them.

The war for San Francisco was now official.

And back in the conference room, a worried and fretful Vincenzo Ciprio was telling his brother underboss, "I don't like it, Tommy. I just don't like it one bit. We just give Crazy Franco more raw power than even *Don* DeMarco has had these past years. I don't like it one bit."

"Relax," Vericci said soothingly. "You think I wasn't up on that idea too? But listen, that crazy bastard has had the old man's ear more and more these past few months. I worry about that, too. Listen. Maybe we finally gave Franco enough rope to tangle himself in, eh? Eh?"

Ciprio chewed the idea for a moment, then he smiled, got to his feet, and took his cadre out of there.

More than one war was brewing in San Francisco.

3: AN HONEST SHOT

She had led him through a maze of back streets
and alleyways, picking her way surely and silently
across the abandoned nightclub belt and into Chinatown.

Bolan had maintained a discreet distance throughout, barely keeping her in sight and varying his track
from one side to the other at erratic intervals.

They crossed Grant Avenue and descended deeper
into the labyrinthine bowels of the western Chinese
section and along a narrow street of storefronts—a
mixed business-residential neighborhood of two and
three story buildings with most of the residential community occupying space above the business.

It was a fringe district at the edge of the main
tourist area, with a sprinkling of gift shops, restaurants, and bars catering to visiting Caucasians jum-
bled in with fantan parlors, shops, and cafes which
obviously serviced the Chinatown residents.

The girl halted between a pair of almost identical
restaurants, threw a quick look over her shoulder, and
abruptly disappeared through a darkened doorway.

Bolan passed on by to the next street intersection,
crossed over, and reversed the route in a careful
recon of the neighborhood, prowling the area for

several minutes to get the lie of the land and scouting for possible shadows on his backtrack.

He found the China Doll waiting for him in an unlighted foyer, a tiny cubicle which barely accommodated the opening of the door from the street. He had a quick impression of pleased oriental eyes, and then she was moving through the musky darkness of the stairway and along the second-floor hall.

She went to a door at the end and fussed about with a key while Bolan quietly scouted that level, counting doors and mentally overlaying the floor plan on his larger picture of the neighborhood.

The girl had the door cracked open and she was standing outlined in a faint light from the other side, waiting for Bolan to join her. Instead he went on up the stairway to scout the third level, and she was waiting patiently in the same position when he completed his recon and joined her at the doorway.

"Are you always so careful?" she asked him in a voice that was quietly sober and exultantly tense all at once.

He said. "I try to be. Do you know why?"

She gave her head a quick little jerk and replied, "Yes, I know who you are. And I am Mary Ching. We are allies, believe that. Will you wait for me here while I bring my friends to talk with you?"

His eyes coldly swept that perfect face and he asked her, "Why should I?"

"You will be safe here," she assured him, matching the coldness of his voice. "And you may find my friends intensely interesting. For intelligence purposes if nothing else."

"How long do I wait?"

"One hour, no more."

41

"Too long," he told her.

She showed him the tiny automatic and hissed, "I could have shot you a dozen times if I had hostile intentions. Trust me for one hour."

He grinned suddenly and said, "Okay. But look— don't go yelling my name around. It attracts crowds."

"I know." She pushed the door full open, smiled and said, "Welcome to my humble pad. See you soon."

Bolan growled, "Yeah," and the girl whisked herself softly along the hallway and disappeared down the stairway.

And then Bolan walked into the most pleasant surprise of the night.

He closed the door and leaned against it, surveying the "humble pad" with a quiet appreciation.

It wasn't exactly luxury—it was just damned good taste—and the little flat above the Chinese restaurant was about as appealing to the senses as any place Bolan had been lately.

There was a lot of red and black, soft lights and softer silks and satins, delicate tapestries and fragile little figurines—nothing overdone but all of it beautifully balanced and blended—a place of quiet dignity and beauty.

It was a one-room affair but there was plenty of walking space, even with abundant furnishings and a cozy corner-kitchenette. A closet-sized bath with a folding silk screen for a door completed the accommodations.

Bolan advanced to the center of the room and placed the machine-pistol on a small table ... and then he received a second surprise, this one a bit more jolting.

A sectional couch had been split and cornered against the far wall ... and each section was occupied by a sleeping girl. Both were Caucasians, blonde, apparently young, and huddled beneath light blankets.

Bolan would have been more comfortable with a discovery of a wide-awake crew of Mafia headhunters.

His inner debate was resolved at about the second heartbeat and he was spinning about to quit that place when a tousled blonde head lifted itself from a pillow and a pair of cool blue eyes raked him from stem to stern. A pleasantly modulated, but sleepy voice declared, "Far out."

Soothingly he said, "Relax, wrong door, I guess. I'm leaving."

The voice was wide awake now and teasing as it warned, "Keep on leaving and I'll start screaming."

"I thought this was Mary Ching's place," he explained.

"It is. What are you made up for? That is really far out."

He said, "Mary didn't say anything about roommates. I'll wait for her outside."

"Don't be square." The girl flung back the blanket and sat up, swinging her feet to the floor. She was wearing nothing but glowing skin, and doing that quite beautifully.

Bolan could have been a lifesized poster, for all the feminine awareness she was according his presence.

"We don't live here," she told him. "We're just crashing for the night. So don't leave on our account."

She shivered and drew the blanket over the bare shoulders.

43

"Make some tea or something, huh?" she suggested lazily.

Bolan said, "I guess that's your department."

She told him, "Monkeyshit," in a quietly disgusted voice and lunged across to slap the other girl's upraised behind.

That one whimpered and burrowed deeper into her blanket.

The live one struggled to her feet and crossed to the bathroom, her blanket draped carelessly from the waist and trailing along behind. She left the folding screen ajar and straddled the toilet seat, staring curiously out at Bolan as she noisily disturbed the waters of the porcelain bowl.

He turned away and decided, hell, to make the tea after all. He put a kettle of water on the burner and rummaged through the cupboard, finding and deciding upon a jar of instant coffee.

"No tea, just coffee," he called in to the blonde.

She was bent over the wash basin, now, splashing water on her face and gasping with the coldness of it. "Is it organic?" she called back.

Bolan muttered to himself, "How the hell would I know?"

She strode into the room, *sans* blanket and patting at her face with a small handtowel.

Bolan, what the hell, looked her over and liked what he was looking at. Any man would. She had those flowing lines and flawless skin that a guy associates with erotic fantasies, large swollen breasts with the pinkest nipples Bolan had seen anywhere, firm and erect as any plastics job could assure—one of those ripple-soft bellies plunging into velvet thighs and belled hips, a swooped rear-deck with the soft overhang visible even from the front.

Sure. She had it all, right where it belonged and in ideal portions.

"If it isn't organic I wouldn't touch it," she was telling him.

Again Bolan turned away from her and fiddled with the stove. He didn't know about the coffee crystals, but Bolan himself was sure as hell organic, one hundred percent *male* organic, and it was no time for delectable female pastries to be flaunting themselves at his maleness.

"Honesty," she was saying in that old-young girl's voice. "That's what this sick world needs the most. No deceits, no additives or deductives, just pure organic honesty."

He said, "Yeah, with all the chemicals left out." He could have done without a few male type chemicals himself, at the moment.

When he looked again the towel was lying on the floor of the bathroom and the girl and the blanket had returned to the couch.

She was lying there on her side, an elbow in supporting position and the blonde head elevated and resting on an honest palm. The blanket was riding loosely amidships and not providing much in the way of warmth or security. Just honesty.

He told her, "It's plain old mountain grown Folgers, and if it's good enough for Mrs. Olsen, then it ought to be good enough for anybody. Do you want some or don't you?"

She suggested, "Why don't you come over here and ball me awhile first."

He said, "What?"

45

"Ball. You know."

Bolan poured the steaming water into his cup and growled, "Thanks, not now."

The girl shrugged and said, "Square."

He said, "Sane."

She giggled.

He growled, "Putting me on, weren't you."

"Not all the way. I wouldn't mind if you really wanted to. I mean, what's the hassle? Person to person, that's what life is. Right?"

He said, "I guess so."

"I mean, if you want to slurp and hunch awhile, and if that'll make you happy, then why not? Right?"

He said, "Pure organic honesty, eh?"

"Right. I mean, why get turned off by a shot of honesty? That's what you did. Right? You turned off the minute I started laying it out. I mean, it's natural for girls to pee, you know. All of us do. So why do it behind closed doors? Right?"

"I guess it's a matter of conditioning," he told her.

"But it turned you off. Can you admit that?"

He smiled. "Maybe."

"Male chauvinist pig," she said lightly. It didn't sound as though she meant it.

He fixed her coffee and took it to her. Her eyes thanked him and she asked him, "What's the gig with the weapons of destruction?"

He told her, "I kill people."

She squealed with genuine delight and cried, "Now you're getting with the honesty bag. You don't liberate enslaved peoples, you don't uphold law'n order, you just flat out, honestly, straight from the gut *kill* people. Now I like that."

46

He showed her a wry smile and said, "Sure. It's a bloody gas."

Her eyes widened suddenly and, in an awed tone, she declared, "*Far* out. I know who ... you're that executioner dude. You're. ..."

He said, "I told the China doll I'd wait for an hour. When that hour is up, I'll be leaving. Until then, let's you and I just cool it. I'm not going to hurt you, so just—"

"Far *out!* I was down in the desert last year when you—I saw your picture I guess a hundred times, on television and everything. Hey, I was at that commune down by Twenty Nine Palms. You know the one?"

He shook his head. "No, I. ..."

The blonde had thrown herself half off the couch to reach the sleeping girl, and she was tugging at her blanket and trying to arouse her. "Hey, Panda ... Panda—wake up!"

She won the battle for the blanket and jerked it clear, flinging it across the room.

The other girl was as organically honest—and as esthetically pleasing—as her buddy, but not quite as willing to face the new day. She curled her nudity into a tight ball, hugging her knees and moaning, "Don't, don't, that's not fair, Cynthey, don't do that."

Bolan went over and got the blanket and arranged it over the girl, and he told the other one, "Let her sleep."

She sniffed and said, "That's Panda Bare. Not her real name of course, but it's honest enough for the squares that watch us do our thing. We're actresses. I'm Cynthia. Believe it or not, I'm a star, a real live movie star."

Bolan said, "Congratulations."

"You don't believe me. Have you ever seen *Midsummer Night's Wetdream?*"

He smiled and shook his head in a negative reply.

"How about *Hotpants Honeypot? Three On A Mattress?*"

Bolan said, "No, I guess not."

"They're porno movies, skin flicks. Haven't you ever seen *any?*"

"I guess not."

"I co-starred with Panda in *Three On A Mattress*. She's a lez."

Bolan said, "Do tell."

"Well *I'm* not. Hey! Did you come here to talk to *me?*"

He asked her, "Why would I?"

"Am I working for the fucking Mafia? Is that what you're saying?"

Bolan smiled. "Did I say that?"

"You didn't have to. I've suspected it for a long time now. They're Italians. Everybody in the fucking company is an Italian."

He told her, "So are some of the finest citizens this country has ever produced. A name doesn't mean anything."

The girl smiled and actually dropped her eyes. In a small voice, she said, "I've really turned you all the way off, haven't I."

He said, "Yeah, all the way."

"Well what else can you expect? I mean, that's the kind of broad I am. Right?"

He told her, "I hope not."

"Well ... not deep down. I mean, not down where it really counts. I guess I just got turned off on my-

48

self, huh? I mean, when you ball six or seven hours a day on scummy sheets under bright lights with the whole world watching you . . . well I guess you sort of get turned off on yourself."

Bolan said, "I guess you could."

"We only do it when we need the bread. We—Panda and me—we live over in Sausalito. Us and a bunch of other kids. On a houseboat."

He said, "Okay."

"I haven't had a good ballin' since I started this crummy business. I guess I'm just turned all the way down."

"Too much honesty, maybe," Bolan quietly suggested.

"Huh?"

"Romance is a system of tender deceits. Right? Even the beasts of the field go through courtship rituals. You know?"

She said, "Right, right, I know."

Bolan ended an embarrassed silence with, "Uh, Mary Ching is bringing some people over here in a little while. Maybe you girls would rather not be around during that. It just could get rough."

The girl said, "Right, right. I guess we'd better split."

"Don't, uh, don't mention seeing me, Cynthey. Okay?"

"Right, right."

"I'll go outside and let you girls have some privacy."

"Oh sure. Say, uh . . . Executioner . . . I'll be at the flick studio up on Geary for the next few days, eight to five. If you, uh, have time. . . ."

"I'll try," he promised.

The other girl was watching him over the edge of her blanket. She sat up suddenly, holding the cover close to her, and said, "Cynthey, don't get yourself involved with this guy. You know what he is."

Cynthey was giving Bolen a dewey-eyed look.

He sighed and said, "Both of you keep clear. And if you like Mary Ching, then don't breathe a word linking me to her. It could mean her life. Right?"

He got up and went out, slinging the machine-pistol over his shoulder and blending into the darkness of the hallway to await a meeting with "allies."

The two girls came out a few minutes later and hurried down the stairs. They did not see Bolan and they were arguing about something in angry whispers.

Panda Bare and Cynthia.

Bolan grinned sadly and shook his head.

Yeah. San Francisco was some kind of town.

As he waited in the darkness, he decided that maybe the old city was over-infested with too many diverging ideas of "honesty."

Maybe the golden city could use a bit of romantic deceit, some good, old, common jungle courtship.

He waited there in the dark, took the matter under advisement, and promised himself that he would get to the heart of San Francisco . . . or die trying.

Yeah, he could sure die trying.

4: FRIENDS AND ENEMIES

There were three of them plus the girl, and Bolan waited until all were framed in the light from the open doorway before he made his move.

He came up from the rear with the stuttergun at the ready, and commanded, "Freeze! Hands on the head while I get a look at you!"

There was no argument.

He patted them clean, removing hardware and sending them inside one by one. The girl turned over her tiny weapon without a murmur and went in with a half-smile on her face.

The look of these men, two of them anyway, recalled in Bolan's mind the buried memories of Korea—and those memories were not so pleasant.

There was something about the Chinese that stood them apart from other Asians, especially as fighting men. There was a hardness of the mind there which was reflected in the face, in the way the head rode atop those shoulders—and there was an inherent ferocity of the spirit which Bolan had found in no other Asian nationals.

Yeah, these were fighting men.

The incessant wars of a thousand centuries were burned into their genes.

51

Bolan had learned to respect them in Korea ... and he respected them now.

The third man had moved on beyond that—from warrior to wise man. He dressed as most San Franciscans do—in an all-seasons suit and a light topcoat, and he wouldn't have drawn a second look from the average tourist.

Those who looked twice, though, would discover a man of quiet but tough dignity, and they would look into the eyes that had seen everything to see and learned to accept nothing at face value.

He was an old man—quite old—but he seemed to be in excellent command of mind and body. And there was no doubt that he was also in command of the other two men, the young warriors. They were little more than bodyguards, Bolan decided.

He removed the clip from the automatic weapon and thrust it into his belt, then he dropped the gun to the floor with the others. It was a peace gesture, even though his other weapon was very much in evidence and ready to leap.

"I am Daniel Wo Fan," the old man told him.

Bolan nodded and said, "I am Mack Bolan."

The old boy didn't waste time on preliminaries. He eased onto a chair and told Bolan, "Your enemy is my enemy."

The Executioner said, "Then you have a lot of enemies."

Wo Fan smiled a fragile smile. "You are rapidly reducing their numbers, I am told. We will help you all we can."

"You'll help me best by standing clear," Bolan told him. "Allies get in my way, and I don't like to walk on their backs."

The statement was not given as an insult, nor was it received as one.

"There is more evil in San Francisco, Mr. Bolan, than one man alone can possibly hope to overcome. It goes beyond your *Cosa Nostra.* It embraces not only you and me, but your children and mine and their children after them. It rides the breast of the global seas and glides upon the atmospheres of all the continents, both east and west, north and south."

The old man gave his head that slow mandarin shake of authority. "A warrior without allies will not survive the day in San Francisco, Mr. Bolan. We do not need you. You need us."

And suddenly Bolan knew who Wo Fan was. He was the Chinese equivalent of a *Capo*—the big daddy, probably, of the San Francisco *tongs.* There was a difference, though, and Bolan was trying to pull the thing together in his mind.

The early *tongs*, or Chinese secret societies, had been as influential in their spheres as the Mafia had become in the Occidental world of today. In San Francisco, especially, they'd been the boys with the lotteries, the opium, the prostitution and even actual slavery, the murder shops, and all the other varieties of underground activity in the Chinese community.

Now—if Bolan's intel was on the right track—now Chinatown's vice lords were aligned with the larger mob, the Mafia, and the leadership of the *tongs* had passed into more respectable hands. The secret societies of the Chinese had turned their energies into the constructive side of commerce and politics, and a fresh new wind had been blowing across the Chinese-American landscapes.

A little flag sprang up in the Executioner's mind, a

flag buried there in Las Vegas by his friend Carl Lyons, the undercover cop from L.A.

"*Red China,*" Lyons had said.

"*What?*"

"*Yeah. How's that for a mob combination? And the trade, we hear, is lively.*"

"*In what?*"

"*In everything. It's developing into the largest invisible market in the world.*"

And now Wo Fan was sitting here talking about the evil that rides the seas and hovers above all the continents.

A chill trickled along Bolan's spine, and he told the old one, "I live by the hour, one of them at a time. Every new day I see is an unexpected victory. Whether I live another day or drown in my own blood an hour from now is not the greatest worry of my life. Thanks for your offer, but I have to fight my war my way."

It was a long speech, for Bolan.

Wo Fan seemed to understand that the young soldier was simply trying to get the cards out cold for all to see. He smiled and said, "As you wish."

He went out then, and the bodyguards scooped up their weapons and followed without a glance at Bolan.

Mary Ching hurried out behind them, remained briefly in the hallway, then came back into the apartment and closed the door with a bang.

She was angry, and she was making no effort to conceal the fact.

Bolan told her, "No disrespect intended. Tell him that, when you see him again."

He had retrieved the machine-pistol. He snapped in the clip and moved toward the door.

She cried, "You just hold it right there!"

Bolan turned to her with a tight grin. A bland product of the inscrutable East she was definitely not. She was a good old American girl, as educated and sassy and assertive as any. Bolan liked her. He said, "I've held too long already. Uh, your girl friends crashed out when I crashed in."

"*What* girl friends?"

"San Francisco's gift to the sexually underprivileged. Panda Bare and Cynthia."

Her face reflected a sudden worry. "Oh! I didn't know they were here."

"Yeah, well, take a word from a guy who knows. Move out of this place for a few days. Little girls like to tell big secrets, and you're liable to have a lot of angry visitors before the day is done. I mean it, these guys play very rough games, and I don't think you'd like to be *it*."

She bit her lip and said, "I know."

He had his hand on the doorknob.

Breathlessly, she said, "Please don't go."

"Thanks for all," he told her, and opened the door.

The guy out there was as surprised as Bolan. He'd been tiptoeing along the hall toward Mary Ching's door, and he froze there in the sudden light, balancing on one foot, the eyes flaring in quick consternation.

Bolan didn't know the guy, but he knew the mold he'd been peeled from, and there was no possibility of a mistaken identification.

The torpedo went for his gun, the hand blurring in Bolan's vision as it swept inside the flapping coat.

55

Bolan's mind sliced into one of those flashing command decisions. He went for the silenced Beretta Belle instead of the burpgun, and there was no unnecessary cloth to get in the way.

The Belle leapt clear and tracked-on spitting, reflexively sending her first greeting smashing into the gunhand of the opponent and splattering it, then climbing for the heart and the head—and the *Mafioso* went down gurgling with three Parabellum hi-shock expanders displacing several cubic inches of vital matter.

Bolan stepped over the crumpled remains and ran to the stairwell, listening with quivering attention for the audible signs of another one. Where there was one of these, there were usually two.

Mary Ching lurched through the doorway and stood with her hands to her face, staring down at the dead man.

Bolan made a lunge back along the hall, shoved the girl inside, hissed, "Stay put!"—then quietly closed the door, making his way through the darkness, down the stairs, and across the small vestibule to the street.

The second man was standing directly across the way, barely visible and leaning nonchalantly against a store front.

It looked like a routine stake-out—or maybe simply an outside watch for what was supposed to be an easy inside hit.

Bolan stepped into the open and called over, "Hey!"

The guy jerked upright and almost turned himself around trying to slap some leather. The Belle sent a single silent sizzler across the pointblank range, and the *Mafioso* continued turning into a corkscrew to the sidewalk.

Bolan was there before the corpse could untangle itself. He hefted the dead weight onto a shoulder and carried it along the street to the alleyway, several doors down.

A convenient trash barrel behind a gift shop made the perfect repository. The Executioner left his mess there, then returned quickly to Mary Ching's.

She had disregarded his instructions, and had wrapped the bloodied corpse in a heavy blanket and dragged it inside the apartment.

Bolan found her kneeling over the dead hood, going through his pockets.

She looked up with a frown and, in a faint voice, told Bolan, "I think I know this man. He—it's hard to say for sure, with his head all—like that—but I believe I've seen him at the club. He works for Franco Laurentis."

Bolan muttered, "Crazy Franco."

"That's the one. They called this man Ralph the Pretender. He was one of those cold, silent ones that stand around, see all, and say nothing."

Bolan pulled the girl to her feet and led her to the couch. She was sort of shook up. He guided her down, lit a cigarette, glared at her silently for a moment, then he told her, "Okay, it's time for a talk. What is Crazy Franco's interest in Mary Ching?"

She said, "I ... I believe the interest is in Mr. Wo Fan. Obviously he was followed here."

"Then why didn't the tail stick with him? Why hang around here?"

"I don't know why."

"Maybe Ralph the Pretender came *with* Wo Fan, not behind him. Maybe he hung around outside until the boss left and sent him on up."

57

"That's ridiculous!"

"What makes you so sure of that?"

"It just is. Besides, I. . . ."

"You what?"

"Nothing," she said sullenly. "You can leave now."

"Not yet. What were you doing at the China Gardens tonight?"

"I work there."

"Yeah?"

"Yeah." She dropped her eyes. "Well . . . actually I work for Mr. Wo Fan. We've had the China Gardens . . . under surveillance. For some time."

"Why?"

"They—well you know what they do there."

"Sure. But why should Wo Fan care?"

"He cares about many things."

"Such as."

The dark eyes blazed defiantly. "Such as the dangerous way our government has started leaning toward an accommodation of mainland China."

"Try again," Bolan told her. "That's no reason to be watching Joe Fasco's operation. Is it?"

"There's more reason than you might think," she declared angrily. "The American underworld has been dealing with Red China for some time. Things have been bad enough around here, even with the official embargo on mainland cargoes. What do you think it's going to be like when the legitimate trade routes are opened?"

"I don't know," Bolan admitted. "Educate me."

"There isn't time for a cram course on political science and social economics." Her eyes flashed to the bundle on the floor. "What are we going to do about this dead man?"

Bolan said, "I'll worry about that. What is Wo Fan's immediate problem?"

"All the problems are immediate," she replied coldly. "At the moment, he is trying to assure the survival of the legitimate Chinese business community."

"And things are looking grim?"

The girl was beginning to thaw again. The hint of smile returned to her voice as she told him, "That's about the softest way of putting it."

It was time to twang her again.

He asked, "What were you doing at the China Gardens an hour after the doors closed this morning?"

"I was gathering intelligence."

"Uh huh. Of what nature?"

She glared at him for a moment, then she shrugged and said, "What's the difference? It's all in the fire now."

He said, "Give, dammit!"

"I was tracking a shipment."

"A shipment of what?"

"Counterfeit art treasures. Ming period, supposedly. They are arriving sometime this week."

Bolan did not necessarily believe her, but he went along. "By what route?"

She smiled wryly. "That's what I was about to discover when you blew the place up, Mr. Bolan. Why all the sudden interest? I was getting the idea that—"

"I'm trying to protect your lovely hide, lady. A hired assassin was standing just outside your door a couple of minutes ago. So listen to me now and think carefully before you answer. Can you think of any reason why Franco Laurentis would send a hit man to your door?"

"I . . . I guess not."

"When I first spotted you this morning, you were in a hell of a hurry. Almost as though someone was chasing you. Was there?"

She shook her head. "No. I'm sure I hadn't been seen. I was . . . just. . . ."

"So you've convinced yourself that these two goons were tailing Wo Fan?"

"Yes I—what *two* goons?"

"There was another one waiting across the street," he explained.

"Did you. . . ?"

He nodded. "Clean."

The girl sighed tremulously and showed him a pair of eyes that had taken in one bloody sight too many. She bit her lip and said, "Well I don't know what to think. I'm just about ready to say to hell with the whole thing."

He squeezed her shoulder and told her, "I guess it's too late for that." He pulled her off of the couch and gently nudged her toward the door. "Come on."

"Come on where?"

"We'll think about that on the way. Right now I just want you out of here and a hell of a long ways clear."

"Does that mean that you're going to go on protecting my hide?"

He growled, "For the moment, yeah."

There was also the matter of Ralph the Pretender. Bolan wrapped the remains tightly in the blanket and draped the package over his shoulder.

"Let's go," he said gruffly.

The girl led the way, and they went through the darkened hallway and down the stairs in silence.

The time was nearly five o'clock.

And the night was almost gone.

They were less than twenty paces clear of the street door when a vehicle swung around the corner down-range.

Bolan pressed the girl into the dark entranceway of a store, and they waited for the vehicle to pass. It did not. It came to a halt directly outside Mary Ching's building, and the lights went out.

Bolan cautioned the girl with a finger across her lips, his eyes remaining riveted to the car.

The door opened and a big man slid out to the street. He wore a blue uniform and a badge, and he seemed to know precisely where he was going.

As the big cop disappeared inside the building, Bolan asked the girl, "Did you see him?"

"Yes," she whispered.

"Know him?"

"It looked like Barney Gibson."

"And who is Barney Gibson?"

"He's the head cop at Harbor Precinct. At the moment, anyway."

"Friend of yours?"

"Not exactly."

They moved on, quickly, detouring via the alleyway so that Bolan could deposit Ralph the Mess, and then they headed straight for Russian Hill.

It was developing into a hell of a hit.

5: PARAMETERS FOR COMBAT

Any visitor to the city who has ever taken the fabulous cable car ride from Powell and Market to Fisherman's Wharf has had an experience not difficult to remember . . . and that final drop from Russian Hill, down Hyde Street to the Bay, is a spectacular finale befitting the adventure.

From atop the hill most of the north bay is laid out in a panoramic sweep from the Golden Gate to the Embarcadero, with views of Fort Mason, Aquatic Park, Alcatraz Island, and—on a clear day—across to the rugged backdrop of Marin County.

For a luckless traveler afoot in the mist-laden darkness of the early morning, however, Russian Hill presents merely another muscle-straining obstacle in a city of obstacles—and Mack Bolan was finding himself no exception to the rule.

This combat-zone athlete's heart was thudding against his ribcage and his breathing was becoming an ordeal by the time he steered Mary Ching through the gateway to his "drop"—a large, old home on the north slope which had long ago been converted to an apartment building—and which was a few short blocks removed from the mansion of *Don* Roman DeMarco.

"That's the last time I walk across *this* town," he panted.

The girl leaned against him for support, breathing too hard for comment. He pulled her to the rear of the building and they paused there, getting their breath and allowing overtaxed muscle tissues a chance to relax.

Presently she asked, "What ... are we doing ... back here?"

He pointed to the fire escape, hovering just above their heads. "My private entrance," he told her.

"Are we ... breaking in?"

"No. My humble pad is up there. Top floor."

She groaned and rolled her eyes and told him, "Okay. If you can, I can."

Bolan chuckled and made a leap for the raised platform. The hinges creaked a little but the contraption came down with his weight, and he ushered the girl aboard with a flourish.

His window was open exactly two inches, the shade drawn to an inch above that—precisely the way he had left it. Still ... Bolan had not survived this long on sloppy security.

He moved his lips to Mary's ear and whispered, "Stay!" Then he quickly raised the window and slid inside.

She was becoming worried and fidgety when finally the lights came on inside. A moment later Bolan's smiling face appeared at the window and he said, "Okay."

He helped her in, then lowered the window and shuttered it.

The girl was looking around, wrinkling her nose as only a scrutable Chinese doll can do it.

He said, "Well it's not sable and satin, I'll agree."

Mary was still having trouble with her breathing. She said, "No ... I was just wondering if you always come home so carefully."

He shrugged and showed her a grin. "Just another small sacrifice of warfare," he said lightly. "Uh ... kitchen's that way. Why don't you brew us some coffee? I have a phone call to make."

She said, "You actually set up housekeeping here?"

"It's safer this way."

She replied, "I guess it is," and went on to the kitchen.

Bolan dropped onto a threadbare couch that groaned under his weight. He lit a cigarette and allowed the smoke to surge around inside for a moment, then he coughed and reached for the telephone.

It was a long-distance, operator-assisted call to a number on the far side of the country.

The timing, he figured, would be just about perfect.

He got the connection on the third ring and the operator was announcing, "San Francisco calling Mr. Frank LaMancha."

The responding voice was gruff and seemingly unimpressed with a call from the Golden Gate. "You got the wrong number, honey," it reported. "There's no LaMancha here."

The operator went through the formality of verifying the number. The man assured her that indeed she had gotten the number she'd dialed, but he still didn't know anybody named LaMancha.

Bolan heard the decisive click of that instrument nearly three thousand miles away. His own voice had never entered the connection. The operator told him, "I'm sorry, sir. Would you like to refer to Pittsfield information?"

He replied, "Thanks, I'll check my own book."

He hung up and studied his watch. It was 5:30. It would be 8:30 in Pittsfield. He looked up to find the China doll studying him from the kitchen doorway.

"Your kitchen is a mess," she told him.

"Find the coffee okay?"

She nodded her head. "Make your call?"

He said, "No good. Try again in five minutes please."

She smiled. "Thank you, Mack."

"For what?"

"For bringing me here. For ... trusting me. I know what it must be costing you—in your own peace of mind."

He grinned and told her, "That's one of war's nicer sacrifices."

"I guess I always pictured ... men like you ... as living high on the hog. You know. Luxury hotel suites, flashy broads lying all around hot and naked, gourmet food and vintage wines, all that."

Bolan shook his head. "That's the enemy you're thinking of."

She said, "Well does this crash pad come equipped with john?"

He smiled. "Off the bedroom, and watch out for the roaches."

She made a face at him and disappeared.

Bolan smoked and watched the time tick by. At 5:35 he again picked up the phone, but this time he poked out a direct-dial to a public telephone which was located several Pittsfield city blocks from the home of Leopold Turrin, a *caporegime* in Bolan's home town, scene of the original conflagration point of this impossible damned war.

One of the nicer surprises of the Pittsfield battle was the last-second revelation that Leo Turrin was an undercover cop.

It was friends like Leo that made the war a bit less impossible ... but just a bit less.

They had worked out the telephone routine for contacts which would not jeopardize the security of either.

Bolan got his response this time on the first ring.

A hell of a comforting sound said, "Yeah, hello."

Bolan said, "Avon calling."

"Well at least you didn't drag me out in the middle of the night this time. Hey ... *paisano* ... get the hell out of that Goddamned town."

"Can't. Not yet. The irons are hot."

"That's not all that's hot. The wires are burning from coast to coast, and they're all screaming one thing. Death to Bolan. You picked a bummer this time, buddy."

"They're all bummers. The word is already out back there, eh."

"Hell, hours ago."

"The mob's telegraph gets better all the time."

"The first word didn't come from that side of the street."

"No?"

"No is right. The fuzz wires were burning minutes after your hit. Well, maybe an hour after. Ever hear of a James Matchison. *Captain* James Matchison?"

"No. Should I?"

"You should, and I'm betting you will. He heads up

66

a specialty outfit in the soggy city, geared for open warfare and committed to the salvation of San Francisco. It's called the Brushfire Squad, and they've elected you their next triumphal achievement. They're not going to give you the keys to the city, Sarge."

"I don't want the keys, just the garbage franchise."

"They're going to bury you in their garbage, friend."

"Did Matchison tell you that personally?"

"He did."

"They actually contacted you?"

"Via the usual routine, yeah. I'm the quote foremost *living* authority unquote on Mack the Bastard. The guy wants your blood, Sarge. I could smell his tastebuds at three thousand miles. Take my advice and get out."

"What did you tell him?"

"The usual honest truth, what else."

"Okay, I'll take a helping of that, too. Give me a rundown on Daddy DeMarco. What are his pet things here?"

"The usual stuff."

"Tell me something unusual."

Turrin sighed across the wire. "One of these days, my buddy, my fuse is going to get lit from both ends and I'm going to go up in a puff of police outrage and mob vengeance. Why can't you just say hi, how's the weather, how's your heart beating, and let it go at that."

Bolan said, "Okay. How's your heart beating, Leo?"

The cop/*Mafioso* chuckled and replied, "Same as ever. Uh, you're looking for a fresh handle, eh?"

"Yeah. The boys are starting to treat me with respect. Soon as I hit town, everything grinds to a halt."

"Yeah, well, that's per official directive from the commissioners. You're going to be getting that from now on."

"Well ... "

"You might look at an outfit calling itself Baysavers, Incorporated."

"*What* are they saving?"

"The San Francisco Bay, among other things. Can you imagine the mob getting ecology conscious?"

Bolan said, "Sure. They've been fighting the overpopulation problem for years."

Turrin chuckled and said, "They're fighting industrial pollution now."

"Then there must be a buck in it somewhere," Bolan replied.

"There's the secret. There are plenty of bucks in it."

"Nothing's sacred, is it."

"Just *omerta*. Uh, you know about Thomas Vericci?"

"Tom the Broker."

"Yeah. He's an invisible director of Baysavers ... and not always so invisible. The feds are poking into it, but they can't prove anything yet. Meanwhile several formerly profitable bay-area industries have been forced into receivership, and at least two of them have wound up in Vericci's other pocket."

"Which side of the street does this intel come from?"

"The police side. We hear very little, really, from the west coast arms. *We* meaning the mob. They run their own cozy little shops out there, with as little contact with the national council as they can get away with."

"Yeah, so I've heard. Okay. It sounds pretty vague, but maybe I'll look at Baysavers."

"Do it easy. The words I get, Vericci got a bunch of kids conned into the act. Naider's Raiders types. They think they're saving the bay for the fishes. I guess they don't know about the sharks they're running with."

"I get the picture," Bolan said. "Speaking of pictures, what do you know about porno movies?"

The man in Pittsfield chuckled merrily. "Not as much as I'd like to know. Which end are you talking about?"

"What ends are there?"

"Well ... you've got distributors and you've got exhibitors. Some of the boys have been active in both areas, from time to time."

"Who makes the movies?"

"Nowadays, just about everybody. They're legit in most places."

"This could be important, Leo. Do you know of any of the boys in this area who might be making these movies?"

"No, not offhand. I could look into it, but it would take awhile."

"I guess I don't have awhile."

"Okay. Anything else on your mind?"

"What can you tell me about the ChiComs?"

Turrin whistled softly. "Nothing."

"Nothing at all??"

"That's right. I keep hearing Red China rumors, but it all sounds pretty wild. I wouldn't even repeat such crap, not even to you."

"Okay. How about Mr. King?"

"Hell, you do jump around. What about Mr. King?"

"Who is he, really?"

"I wish I knew. So do ten thousand feds. Speaking of them, you're on their shit list, buddy. Especially after Haiti. The men up high are actually frothing at the mouth, I hear."

"Sorry if I embarrassed them," Bolan said drily. "But a hit is a hit."

"Well, they did have some bad moments. Haiti is an OAS member, you know. And with all the rumors floating around that you're actually being sponsored by everybody from the FBI to the CIA ... well, it got pretty messy."

Bolan laughed out loud.

"Don't laugh," Turrin said. "Even some of the congressmen are starting to wonder if you're sponsored. The feds are going to have to burn you, buddy, just to prove the rumors wrong."

"About Mr. King," Bolan prompted, changing the subject.

"Hell I told you, I don't know. I guess there aren't more than two or three men in the whole country who know his true identity. The name has been falling out of tapped telephones for years, and everybody generally agrees that he pulls the strings all over the western states ... but hell that's it, Sarge. There just simply isn't any make on the guy. And he's not Mafia, he's bigger than that."

"I hear that *Don* DeMarco is his pipeline into the mob. I hear that's what *made* DeMarco, and that's what's keeping him made."

There was a long pause, then Turrin replied, "You've

70

got better ears than mine, then. I never heard anything like that."

"Okay. Thanks a bunch, Leo."

"You, uh, don't want to know about anybody else?"

"You know I do." Bolan's voice went softly serious. "How are they?"

The reference was to Bolan's sole surviving relative—the kid brother, Johnny. And to Valentina Querente, Bolan's warmest love, the schoolteacher who'd taken over the care and feeding of young John.

"They're fine," Turrin reported. "The kid keeps a scrapbook on you. He's going to be wanting to join you some day, Sarge . . . if you should live so long. I mean . . . he wants a piece of your war. If you're still around by then."

"Don't worry," Bolan said tightly. "I won't be. Their security still okay?"

"Yeah. First class. Uh, Val keeps agitating for a meet. She's, uh—"

"Tell Val I'm dead, Leo. Tell her to find herself a nice, clean history teacher or something and settle down to the good life."

"I've told her a hundred times, Sarge."

"Well keep telling her. She's an old maid already. Tell her I said that."

"Okay, but it won't do any good. She's a Rock of Gibraltar, you know that."

"It's just a matter of time anyway," Bolan muttered.

"Yeah. She knows that. And she's prepared for it. But she does want to see you, Sarge. One last time, she says. One hour, she wants one hour."

"I don't have one," Bolan said miserably.

"I know, I know."

"Leo. Thanks. You're a—"

"Yeah, yeah, shut up."

"So long."

"So long, dead man. Call me any time you can."

"I will."

Bolan hung up and lit another cigarette. He stared at the telephone for a moment, then he sighed and went looking for the China doll.

The coffee was boiling over on the stove. He took it off.

She wasn't in the bedroom.

The bathroom was empty.

Mary Ching was not there.

The China doll had taken a powder.

6: POINT OF CRISIS

So, she'd taken off.

So, what the hell, it was her right. She owed Mack Bolan nothing, he owed her nothing, and the quiet disappearance did not necessarily classify her as one of the enemy.

Of course, though, it could.

A whole host of threatening possibilities were standing there at the edge of Bolan's mind . . . Mary Ching could very well turn into the greatest threat San Francisco had to offer him.

The only thing that he was certain of was that she *had* left of her own will. She had not been dragged out of there. She had simply released the safety chain, opened the door, and walked away. All the signs attested to that.

But . . . had she left there as friend or enemy?

Either way, there was no good reason why he should continue his residency of that Russian Hill apartment. It had served all his purposes, and now it had quite suddenly become more of an ominous liability than an asset.

And, as suddenly, Bolan was very tired. It was a weariness not of the flesh, but of the inner man—and the inner man had just about had it.

It was that special brand of weariness often known by a man who is called upon to stand too tall, for too long a time, and too utterly alone.

If there had just been someone else—anyone else—to whom he could say, "Okay, that's it. I've had it for now. *You* take over for awhile."

There was no one like that.

There was no hole deep enough to hide him for more than a brief moment, no sanctuary to embrace him in safety from the largest manhunt in history—there was no God damned place to go, except *out to fight.*

And Bolan was sick of the sight and smell of blood.

He was wearied with worrying about all the incidental non-combatants who straggled across his battlefield.

And he was fed up with looking at every other human being as a potential jackal who might rip the flesh off of him.

He was tired of mistrust and suspicion—humbled by the reminder that he was just a man, after all—and thoroughly shaken by the idea that he had an entire city to conquer ... and not just any city but this particular city.

So ... what the hell. It was just another jungle, after all, San Francisco was.

The same rules applied in every jungle.

Kill that enemy son of a bitch, *kill him now* before he has a chance to do it to you.

Bolan's stomach rolled, and he instinctively understood what was happening to him. It was one of those defense mechanisms of the soul, one of those alert little angels of the inner being that kept sounding the alarms whenever the animal in there became too large, too strong, and too difficult to handle.

It had happened before.

It would happen again ... if he lived that long.

It was a point of crisis, he understood that, a crisis of the inner man. But it wasn't a matter of fear or cowardice; it was simply a deep, deep revulsion of what he was doing, of what he had become.

Puke it up, then. Puke it out of your system, Bolan, and then get back out there and *fight*.

He'd done it in Korea. He'd done it several times in Vietnam. And he'd been doing it quite regularly ever since Vietnam.

Okay. The enemy had not defeated him yet. The righteous wrath of the law had not defeated him yet. He was damned if he was going to defeat himself.

We are the hollow men
We are the stuffed men
Leaning together.

That line from T.S. Eliot flashed across Bolan's struggling consciousness, and he knew immediately that his inner man had not yet given up the fight.

Call it a subliminal awareness, or call it the computer-like ability of the human brain to reason effectively, or call it that inner angel—Bolan didn't give a damn what anyone called it.

It had provided his answer, and at a time when he needed one the most. And it was not just an answer to himself. It was an answer, also, to the enemy.

Bolan was not leaning together with anyone.

He stood alone—and, of course, that was the only way to fight his kind of war.

The enemy, though—the enemy were the hollow men, the stuffed men, leaning together.

75

He would, by God, see how well *they* could stand
alone.

The warwagon had been stowed away under tight
security in a rented garage a block away, and it was
here that Bolan had gone without further dalliance.

The little Ford Econoline van was outfitted with
everything required to wage war. It was, in fact, a
rolling arsenal. Bolan was not only a highly trained
warrior—he was also a master gunsmith and a munitions expert. He could build weapons, modify them,
refine them, and improvise a variety of deadly combi-
nations—and he knew how to put all of them to their
best use.

Bolan was, in the literal sense, a one man army. He
alone was the strategist, the tactician, the logistician;
he was G-2, scout, recon patrol, armorer, medic and
warrior.

And it was time to get this war in gear.

Bolan's nights had gone into a surveillance of the
China Gardens. But his days had mostly been spent
on the roof of the "drop"—in excellent binocular command of the DeMarco mansion. He had watched
doors, windows and grounds. He had timed arrivals
and departures of visitors and of tradesmen; he
had made careful notes of the placements and
routines of the palace guard; and he had sketched
layouts of the probable floor plans for all three levels
of the joint. He knew where and when DeMarco
slept; he knew where he ate, and a couple of times he
had even known what.

And now he was going to bust that joint.

Not wide open, not all the way. All he wanted at

the moment was a visible crack or two here and there in the defenses.

He wanted to show DeMarco how hollow he really was.

The warwagon had a shiny new decal on each side. It was now "Bay Messengers, Inc."—and it had been since a few hours after the arrival in the bay city.

That van had been in the DeMarco neighborhood at least twice each day for the past three days; the driver, a tall man in Levi denims and a white windbreaker, had even attempted to make a parcel delivery to the DeMarco house; it was a mistake, of course —no one by the name of "Lamancha" lived at that address.

At any rate, the DeMarco palace guard had acquired at least a passing familiarity with Bay Messengers.

And now Bay Messengers was going to give them a chance to get better acquainted.

Bolan got into the denims, pulling them on over his blacksuit, and slipped into the nylon windbreaker. Then he carefully stuck on a false mustache and pulled a billed cap low over his forehead.

Most people, even sharp-eyed mob people, were not too much on faces when things appeared to them out of the usual context. Sure, anyone would recognize the Executioner in his combat blacks. But to most of the world Bolan's face was no more than an artist's sketch seen in newspapers and magazines, and maybe a few times on television—and the human eye tended to identify things by setting, role, and other general characteristics.

Mack Bolan was a master at what he termed "role camouflage."

He had developed the art in Vietnam and perfected it in such places as Pittsfield, Palm Springs, New York, and Chicago.

It had not let him down yet.

The choice of weapons was the next consideration.

The Beretta would, of course, be at the top of that list. But he needed a grabber, a heavy punch, something that would not unnecessarily encumber him, something that . . . .

His decision focussed around the newest thing in the Bolan arsenal.

He had field-tested the thing two days earlier, and found it awesome.

It came in a handsome little attache-type case and it was such a new item that factory ammo was not yet available. For this honey, Bolan had taken the time to make his own ammo.

It was called "the .44 Auto Mag" and it was the most powerful going in hand guns. It was three and a half pounds of stainless steel—yeah, stainless steel—and measured overall eleven and a half inches. A guy with a small hand wouldn't want to get involved; it took a big strong hand to cope with the recoil from more than a thousand foot-pounds of muzzle energy, and especially long fingers for a comfortable grip and trigger-squeeze.

The Auto Mag had been designed primarily as a hi-punch hunter's handgun, and she'd drop anything that the heavy rifles would bring down in most big-game situations. Bolan had experimented with different loads, and he'd finally settled for a combination of twenty grains of powder charge behind a 240 grain bullet, for damn near 1400 fps of muzzle velocity and a performance uniformity that was really outstanding.

At twenty-five yards the big bullets tore up a one-inch bull in rapid fire, and with a two-hand stance he'd grouped a full clip of those blitzers into an area the size of a man's heart at a range of one hundred yards.

Amazing, yeah.

It was a hell of an impressive looking weapon, too—all silver with ventilator ribs across the top of the barrel—she looked, in fact, just mean as hell, and this was one of the reasons Bolan selected the Auto Mag for the mission. The psycho warfare was almost as important as the other.

The Beretta was sighted in for a pointblank range of twenty-five yards; Bolan had the Auto Mag worked in for precision targeting at one hundred yards; between the two he figured he had a good one-two punch capability.

And there would be no dangling weapons on shoulder straps, nor any of the usual encumbrances of big-punch arms.

He shoved the Auto Mag into the waistband of his denims and concealed the overhang beneath the windbreaker.

So ... he was ready.

Russian Hill was ready.

Bolan just hoped to hell that Mary Ching would not be found among the enemy.

Either way, Bolan had survived another crisis point. He was coming out shooting.

7: TIGER OF THE HILL

Tony Rivoli Jr. was literally born into the DeMarco Family. His father, before him, had been captain of the palace guard through most of the early family history. The elder Rivoli had come west with DeMarco to stake out the virgin territory and he'd been the *Don's* trusted companion and personal gun during those bitter years of war, intrigue and the establishment of empire.

Big Tony had taken a DeMarco niece as his wife, and Little Tony had always regarded the mansion on Russian Hill as his natural home. He was born in the big oval bedroom on the third floor; later that entire level of the house had been converted into an apartment for the Rivoli sub-family. Little Tony still lived there—alone now, except for the steady parade of San Francisco's finest flesh, whom he managed to smuggle in while the old man slept.

Anna Rivoli, Little Tony's mother, died of natural causes one week following her only child's tenth birthday. Quiet household gossip insisted that she "drank herself to death." Big Tony was killed in a gun battle with a rival outfit in the early fifties, almost two years to the day later.

From that moment forward, Little Tony Rivoli's life

had followed a curious pattern. The *Don* never public-
ly recognized him as a blood relative. He was always,
"My old friend Tony Rivoli's kid ... little Tony." But
DeMarco had gone through the formalities of having
himself legally declared the boy's guardian. He'd giv-
en him a home, an education, and later a position in
the official household. But there was no warmth between the two, no obvious family ties, and certainly
no hint or suggestion that little Tony would one day
share in the DeMarco estate.

In fact the old man frequently reminded Rivoli that
his "good fortune" depended entirely upon the *Don's*
continued good health.

"That gun there was your papa's best friend, Little
Tony," the old man liked to remind him. "It's yours,
too, you know. That's the blood between you'n me,
and don't you forget it. When I lose the need for your
gun, then we've lost our common bond. You better
remember that and you better stay on your toes. And
you for damn sure better keep me alive as long as you
can. 'Cause when I go, Little Tony, every damn thing
you got in this world goes with me."

Rivoli was twenty-five when first he heard the
whispered story that his father's death had been,
perhaps, an unnecessary event. There had been ten-
sions in the official family, rivalries, and a jockeying
around for power—pressure from without and stress
from within. As the story goes, *Don* DeMarco had
begun to suspect the loyalty of Big Tony—and he had
sent his house captain and old friend out on a personal hit purely as a test of that loyalty. And he had sent
him into a "set-up"—an ambush from which there was
no possibility of return.

Curiously enough, this rumor served only to intensify Little Tony's loyalty to the *Don*—as though he were trying to prove by his own example that the old man had been wrong about his father. This was supposed to explain why Tony Rivoli Jr. had become the tiger of the DeMarco palace guard. Certain members of the official family had their private reservations about this explanation, and they would quietly express their own ideas about Tony Rivoli's tigerhood to anybody but the tiger himself. Whatever the background, Little Tony was elevated to full captaincy in a formal "blood and kisses" ceremony on the eve of his thirtieth birthday, and he had been the militant spirit of DeMarco House ever since.

Nobody except *Don* DeMarco now called him "Little Tony" to his face. The tag had become a ridiculous one, anyway. The "House Tiger" stood just under six feet tall and weighed close to two hundred pounds. Hardened gunmen became nervous under his casual stare, and visiting dignitaries treated him with cordial respect.

It was common knowledge among the palace guard that Mr. Rivoli had "a mean streak"—especially concerning his women. He never had any particular woman more than once, and frequently his "victims" were carried out in the dead of night—bloodied and whimpering. Only once had an official complaint been brought against him in this regard, and on this instance the complainant had failed to show up in court. She had, in fact, failed to show up anywhere, ever.

At the time of Mack Bolan's smash into San Francisco, Tony Rivoli was thirty-three years of age, which put the two tigers into roughly the same age group. Bolan was not much taller and no heavier than the

Tiger of Russian Hill. Each had come into a certain formidable reputation for ferocity and dedication to a cause. But these similarities met only on the surface of the men.

Mack Bolan's savagery was directed only upon the savages of his society. Tony Rivoli's ferocity seemed to be an inherent part of his inner nature, and it was directed primarily into a defense of savagery as a way of life.

On that morning following the strike against North Beach, Rivoli's tiger force was under full alert. The tiger himself had been up the entire night to personally supervise the defense arrangements, and he greeted the arrival of daylight as an unwelcome intrusion into this highly stimulating game of suspense.

He had been hoping that Bolan would come on in and make a grab for the old man. Nothing in Rivoli's secret fantasies would have provided more entertainment than to have Mack Bolan at his mercy.

Tony Rivoli, of course, did not know the meaning of mercy. It was a nonexistent quality of human relations that strong men grovelled for and ended up screaming for. But it was something which Tony Rivoli had never in his entire lifetime actually dispensed—neither in fact nor in fantasy. In the tiger brain of Tony Rivoli, mercy was simply a fantasy of the weak, and nothing would give him more real pleasure than to reduce Mack Bolan to one of those screaming pulpy lumps of whimpering flesh.

He would take him alive, of course. All of his gunners had been solemnly informed that the man who killed Mack Bolan would get a bullet in each knee. Rivoli wanted the bastard *alive*—alive and whole and sweating and dreaming of mercy, yet knowing all the while that there would be no mercy.

The defenses had been set up with that very idea in mind. Nothing obvious. Hell no, don't scare the bastard away. Let him think it would be easy—as easy as that hit on Dum-Dum Fasco at the China Gardens. Let him think it would be waltz job, a quick in and a quick out like he'd always had. He would find it a quick *in*, sure. That's exactly where they wanted him, *in*. But the only way out would be through Tony's playroom on the third floor—and he would find that a worse way than none at all. Yeah, they'd take the bastard alive, all right.

Had Bolan ever heard of the Tiger of Russian Hill?

Probably not.

Tony Rivoli was a family secret. He had never been in jail, never been questioned by any of those crime commissions or any of that jazz, never been mentioned in the press or "exposed" by those jerk magazines.

No. Bolan the Quick would be expecting the routine, run of the mill sort of palace defense. Like old man DiGeorge had down at Palm Springs. A bunch of punk-ass kids who'd never shot anything but the bull's-eye out of a target, and some tired old men who should've stepped aside years ago.

Bolan the Jerk had never run in on a real Tiger defense.

And the tiger of this hill wasn't tipping his hand to the jerk. He just wished the guy had come on in that night, while everybody was up for the job, while his boys were primed and trembling with the anticipation of bagging the biggest game that ever hit this town. Yeah.

So what the hell. The guy would show. Rivoli was

84

positive that the guy *would* show. This was the palace, wasn't it? There was no secret about that. The guy would come. He was just being cagey, cautious, keeping them waiting; thinking that maybe the defenses would get too uptight, maybe over-anxious and careless.

Tonight, probably, would be the night. The guy could even try a daylight hit. But in San Francisco? Right here at the top of the town? With two damned cops per square foot all over the place?

Probably not.

Rivoli checked the time. It was a little past eight o'clock. It was daylight. The old man had gone back to bed. How could he go to bed at a time like this? Bolan might be out there somewhere, watching the joint, checking it out. He could be.

Now if the boys just didn't get uptight and. . . .

The Tiger went out through the French doors to the garden-patio and casually circled the grounds. The fog was lifting. It was now holding at about rooftop level, but the air below it was still saturated with moisture, cold, uncomfortable. Miserable goddam crap! The outside boys would be getting stiff and disgruntled if this kept up.

Rivoli made a mental note to make hourly shifts. As unobtrusively as possible, he would have to rotate those boys between the cars and the open-air stakeouts. The inside boys stayed inside, period and bullshit. There would be no juggling around with those hard boys inside.

A police car went by out front, cruising slowly, and the sight of it disrupted the Tiger's chain of thought. He frowned and headed that way. Those jerks would scare the guy off. Imagine, patrolling in a marked cruiser. How dumb could a cop get? Were they *trying* to scare the guy away?

As he reached the front of the big house, Rivoli noted that a delivery van was standing at the curb down by the service gate, and a guy was coming out of the van with a clipboard under his arm.

Cool it, goddammit, cool it! Don't go slapping that guy up against the fence and frisking him, f'Christ's sake!

The Tiger hurried forward to personally supervise the reception of the deliveryman, groaning inwardly with the certain feeling that the two gatemen were going to over-react—and that those cops in the cruiser would nose into the act. One thing Tony did not need at this point was cops swarming all over the place and asking a lot of jerky questions.

His worries were apparently an over-reaction within himself, though, and this he discovered as soon as he was within earshot of the service gate.

Apparently the boys knew this guy, this delivery jerk. He was a tall guy wearing Levi's and a white jacket, and Rivoli himself had seen the Bay Messengers truck around the neighborhood. The guy had shoved his hat back away from his forehead, and he was grinning and scratching the bridge of his nose with a pencil.

Jerry the Lover Aspromonte was jawing around with the guy through the closed gate, obviously kidding him about something, and Rivoli caught the scrap of a comment, " ... told you the other day, meathead, LaManchas don't live here."

The guy sort of giggled and told Jerry the Lover, "Aw shit, ain't you ever gonna let me live that down?"

"Shit it ain't my fault you can't read th' fuckin' addresses," Aspromonte was saying when Rivoli got there.

"I got it right this time," the guy insisted, with a pleading glance at the new arrival. "You gonna take the damn package or ain't you?"

Tony Tiger didn't give a damn about this jerk and his small worries. The cop car, sure as hell, had come to a complete halt and the dummies were idling there beside the van and ogling the little exchange at the fence.

Rivoli angrily punched the electronic lock and swung out through the gate, causing the delivery jerk to dance back out of the way. The Tiger crossed the street and leaned into the cruiser.

"You guys need something?" he inquired quietly.

One of the guys in there was a fucking spade. In plain clothes, at that. He showed Tony an ivory smile and told him, "Routine patrol, Mr. Rivoli. Don't you be concerned—we have the entire neighborhood under surveillance."

Where the hell did these guys get off, dropping his name around that way? How did that black bastard know what his name was?

Rivoli muttered, "Why the hell should I be concerned about anything?" He whirled around and crossed back to the other side of the street.

The delivery jerk was standing there, arms crossed over his chest, grinning at him with that fuckin' *paisano* mustache curling down over his upper lip and into his mouth. He probably sucked on it, he probably liked the taste of hair in his teeth.

Rivoli snarled, "What the hell are you smiling at, guy?"

The smile froze and the jerk just stood there. He mumbled something about just trying to do his job, then he turned back to Jerry the Lover and said, "Hey, take the package, eh?"

"What is this great big worry you got there, guy?" the Tiger growled.

"I got a delivery for a Tony Rivoli, in care of Roman A. DeMarco. It's this address, I got the right address, but this guy won't get serious. He keeps telling me LaManchas don't live here, just because I—"

"Okay okay, whatta you mean you got a delivery? What kind of a delivery?"

"This little package here, that's all."

The jerk was holding it in the palm of his hand. It was square, like maybe a ring box or something done up in brown wrapping paper.

Rivoli saw the police cruiser in the edge of his vision, moving slowly on along the street.

"Who the hell sent it?"

"Well why don't you just take it and maybe you'll know who sent it. Hell I just run the things around, I just drive the damned—"

Tony the Tiger snatched the package out of the guy's hand and moved on inside the fence.

The guy moaned, "Hey I gotta have somebody sign."

"Sign it and give the jerk a buck," the Tiger instructed Jerry the Lover. Then he went on to the front entrance to the house, fuming inwardly over spade cops who dropped his name around like they had a right to or something.

A *package?*

Who the hell would be sending the Tiger of the Hill

a goddamned *package?* A package of *what?* In all his thirty-three years, no one had ever sent Tony Rivoli a package of anything. Not even on his birthdays. Not even, by God, on Christmas. It couldn't be a damn bomb, it was too small.

It couldn't be a. . . .

Something froze around Rivoli's heart and his fingers trembled slightly as he tore at the wrapping. Too late he had an impulse to yell back to Jerry the Lover to stop that jerk, to hold him there a minute . . . the van was already moving along and cornering onto the street at the side of the house.

Yeah. Yeah, it could be, and it was.

It was a marksman's medal, done up real fancy in a jewelry box with a velvet cushion under it.

The nerve! The *nerve* of that cocky bastard to send it to *him* to give to. . . . The coldness pressed harder upon the Tiger's heart as he realized that *no, no,* it wasn't addressed to the old man at all, it was addressed *in care of* the old man . . . the goddam thing was meant for Tony Rivoli himself!

Where did the wise bastard get his name? Where was everybody suddenly coming up with the Tiger's name, f'Christ's sake!

Rivoli whirled about to shout an instruction to the two gatemen, but the words stuck in his throat. Heavy black smoke was billowing up over there, totally obscuring that area of the yard, and he could not even *see* the damned gate or Jerry the Lover or the other boy or anything but the damned smoke.

In just one fucking second?

Shit, he was hitting! In broad daylight and with cops prowling all around, the nervy bastard was hitting.

Rivoli raced into the yard to give the signal to the upstairs boy, the signal which would be relayed to all the outside boys, to bring them in quietly into a ring of steel around that house, around the whole neighborhood, to seal the smart bastard inside, to cut away all of his running room and even his walking room, to grind him surely and securely within the confines of that house on the hill, and to begin his education into the fantasies of mercy.

And then the Tiger ran on into the smokescreen, to see what the hell had become of the boys at the gate, and to continue wondering why the bastard had sent the mark of death to *him*—why *him?*—why the *Tiger* instead of the *Capo?*

Despite smarting eyes and bursting lungs, Rivoli found the smoke bomb and hurled it across the street. He also found the two boys lying in their own blood, great gaping holes between their eyes, and he found the electric gate standing wide open.

The Tiger staggered clear of the suffocating chemicals and made a run for the front porch. Then he saw the same crap coming up all along that fence, saw it billowing and drifting in a solid cover toward the house itself, saw the new bombs erupting in close sequence and in the exact pattern the goddam Bay Messengers van had taken—and Tony Rivoli began right then and there to re-examine his own fantasies.

The mark of death had come to *him.*

The guy had delivered it personally, and had stood there smiling at him, *laughing at him inside*—that guy with the *paisano* mustache in the Levi's was *Mack Bolan!*

That heavy coldness at the top of Tony Rivoli's heart was the hand of death. He knew it. The guy was

90

there, and he'd come to kill *the defender, not the lord of the manse,* and the Tiger of the Hill was not at all certain now that he'd set the proper defenses for a hit like that.

Hell no, he wasn't sure at all.

"Shoot to kill!" he screamed at the top of his lungs. *"Forget the other stuff!"* God damn you, *all of you, shoot to kill!"*

It was to be a sad lesson in fantasies for Tony the Tiger Rivoli.

8: A MEETING OF TIGERS

Bolan left the van and the excess clothing at the south corner, and he came in with the smoke, over the fence and onto the grounds—a gas-masked, black-clad, striding apparition of doom with a single idea in mind.

It was another numbers game, and he would have to *hit and git* with no unnecessary messing around, or else he would have the law breathing down his withdrawal route.

He crossed the garden-patio and lobbed a fragmentation grenade into a choked and gasping babble of confused voices near the corner of the building; under the cover of that explosion he kicked the French doors open and moved inside with the Auto Mag at the ready. He left the doors open and the smoke came in with him, moving quickly ahead of him and spreading rapidly in an ever-extending blanket of cover.

Thudding feet and an almost hysterical panting signalled the approach of at least two defenders from the front reaches of the house. Someone nearby gasped, "Jeez, get over there and see if those doors are open! The fuckin' place is filling up with smoke!"

Another voice cried, "Bullshit, what was that explosion? I ain't going out there until I know what—"

Then Bolan loomed up from within the swirling smoke, and the two gawked at him in frozen immobility while the Auto Mag roared its throaty message of massive destruction. The two gunners died on their feet while considerable areas of their assaulted anatomy sought a place to settle from the explosively expanding push of the big 240 bullets.

Bolan stepped over the bodies and went on toward the grand stairway, a curving nineteenth century masterpiece of mahogany and marble.

Several someones up-above pumped a wild volley of shots along his path. Again he gave voice to the impressive Auto Mag, in rapid fire, splintering the vertical rungs of a railing up there and sending a fine cloud of powdered plaster drifting along that upstairs hallway.

Someone up there groaned, *"Gee-Zus Christ!"* and the sound of scurrying feet told Bolan that he had them on the run.

He was well along the stairs and feeding a new clip into the Auto Mag when another guy came running in from the foyer.

The guy yelled, "Hey what. . . ?" And then he saw the thing in black on the stairway.

This one's reflexes were working better than the others Bolan had encountered thus far, and a long-barreled .38 revolver was tracking up the stairs and suddenly making a mess of the polished mahogany.

At that distance the guy should not have been missing, but Bolan made allowances for an excited overeagerness, and he covered the guy's embarrassment with 240 grains in the teeth. The gunner's whole head seemed to cave in and fly away. Bolan continued his rush up the stairway.

Another revolver roared and a bullet buried itself into the wall behind his head as he reached the top. He saw a door rapidly open and close at the far end of the hall and—just beyond that—he spotted the window he was looking for.

The lower edge of a brooding layer of cloud strata— the condition they called *fog* in the bay city—was lying just above that window. Below it and trapped, there was a densely churning atmosphere of chemical smoke—a condition called *personnel cover* in the war zones—and Bolan meant to invite it in.

He sent a single shot crashing into the windowglass. It shattered. The Executioner held his position commanding the stairway and patiently waited for the friendly atmosphere to come inside.

An agitated voice down below was announcing to other cautious presences, "He's upstairs I guess, yeah, with a fuckin' cannon or something, I don't know what. Lookit Joey there, just lookit 'im."

"Well where's Mr. Rivoli?" asked another quivering voice.

"I think he's upstairs covering *Don* DeMarco," the other one obligingly revealed.

The Executioner smiled grimly behind his mask, and a two hundred pound package of sudden death merged with the atmosphere of doom and moved unhurriedly into the choking no-man's-land of that upper hallway.

It would have been much simpler, sure, if he'd just taken the guy while he was down there at the gate. But simplicity was not the name of the game.

The idea was to show Big Daddy DeMarco how

vulnerable, how utterly defenseless, how *hollow* he really was.

And once the idea had sunk in that he had no one else to lean against, then maybe. . . .

Yeah, Bolan was betting his very blood on it. *Don* DeMarco would want to lean with Mr. King.

And the Executioner would be content with nothing less.

It was not his idea of fun to terrorize a tired old man of seventy-two. But Roman DeMarco, of course, was not any ordinary old man. With an iron hand he still commanded an empire built of terror and intimidation, savagery and murder—and he could yet turn out to be a formidable foe.

But Bolan would shake this whole damn town apart, if that was what it took.

And he meant to pin a marksman's medal to Mr. King's forehead, whoever and wherever he was. He meant to pin it there with a 240 grain Auto Mag express.

But first ... he had to rattle the house on Russian Hill.

He had to bag himself a tiger, and at the very foot of the throne. He knew precisely where to look.

Sgt. Bill Phillips of the Brushfire Squad was speaking calmly into the radio hookup with his Command Central. "Mark it Hotel Eight on the grid and consider it a positive. It's the DeMarco place on Russian Hill, and if it's not a full assault, then it's at least a probe of some type. He's got them covered up with smoke and—belay that, it's no probe, round one of the artillery war just started. Let's make it a ringer-dinger. Better get some firefighting units up here also."

The voice of the Captain snapped back in a clear staccato. "We're deploying on the grid. Give this character plenty of room, Bill, don't crowd him. Now that's an order."

"Yessir." Phillips sighed and hung up the mike, then he smiled faintly at his white partner. "What he means is, don't blow it," he said quietly.

"He means don't get your head blown off, eager beaver," the other cop replied, chuckling.

"Yeah, well, whatever," Phillips said. He drew his revolver and carefully checked it, then put it away. "They'll be on grid in about two minutes."

The patrolman nodded. "If they get lucky."

"The guy could be halfway to the Golden Gate by then."

A series of booming reports issued from the big house.

The Sergeant's partner grinned and he said, "Not from the sound of that. I'd say he's run into a slight delay."

The black cop lifted a gas mask from the equipment rack. He opened his door and stepped into the street.

The other man said, "Now Bill . . . dammit. . . ."

"I'm just going to cover the front," the Sergeant assured his partner. "Stay with the vehicle." He donned the mask, drew his revolver, and ran toward the booming sounds of open combat.

The black man from Brushfire was going to have himself at least a little piece of World War III.

Bolan opened the door and stepped quickly back, allowing the smoke to precede him into the anteroom of the master suite. Two gunners came staggering out almost immediately, choking, eyes streaming, and their hands clasped atop their heads.

"Keep moving," Bolan advised them. "Down the stairs and down the street, and don't even look back."

One of the men was already bleeding from an arm wound. Both of them hurried down the hall, wheezing, gasping and totally out of the war.

Bolan entered the suite and shot two locks out of a door on the far wall, then he kicked it open.

The smoke puffed on through, and it was met by a spray of slugs that chewed up the door casing and nothing else.

Bolan reached through the opening and fired once at the opposing muzzle flashes.

A gun clattered to the floor and a guy yelled in a high-pitched squeal.

The man in black went on in and closed the door with his foot to keep the polluted atmosphere out.

The *Capo* was standing by the window, swaying slightly and dressed in pajamas and robe. He looked old and sick, and the small amount of smoke that had entered the room had been enough to upset the leathery old lungs.

The Tiger of the Hill stood at the foot of the bed, staring with glazed eyes at the smashed remains of his gun hand. The blood was gushing out and soaking into the bed, and Rivoli was just standing there watching it run.

Bolan removed his mask and told the tiger, "You forgot to sign for the delivery, guy."

The house captain tried to say something in a voice that wasn't working.

The old man croaked, "My God, my God," and he

staggered over to his nephew-once-removed-but-never-acknowledged.

DeMarco took the cloth belt from his robe and made a fumbling attempt to apply it as a tourniquet above the mutilated hand.

His eyes had not yet met Bolan's gaze, and he seemed to be avoiding such a confrontation.

Bolan told the old man, "Save it, DeMarco, he won't be needing that."

Rivoli's lips moved again and he whispered, "No mercy, I said. Shoot to kill. You hear me? Shoot to kill."

Bolan said, "Okay."

He snuggled the Auto Mag beneath the old man's arm and squeezed off once. The big piece roared and bucked against the Capo's chest.

DeMarco lurched forward, eyes wide and stricken with a mortal awareness, and his mouth formed the words, "Missed ... you missed."

Bolan told him, "I never miss," and he walked to the window while he tucked away the Auto Mag and re-fitted the gas-mask to his face.

It was not until then that DeMarco became aware of the mess behind him. The Tiger of the Hill had lost his face plus a goodly portion of skull to the rear ... and the big mean bastard in the black suit had been right about the uselessness of that tourniquet.

Ten thousand tourniquets wouldn't put Little Tony back together again. Pieces of him were splattered all over the bed, even on the walls.

DeMarco yelled, "You bastard you, you bastard! What're you doing this to me for?"

But the window was up, and the bastard was gone, and actually he'd done nothing whatever to *Don* De-

Marco. Except shoot up his house, and fill it with smoke, and splatter Little Tony all over his bedroom, and kill off God only knew how many of the house boys.

The *Don* went over to the window and closed it. He got the hell away from it quick and staggered back to the bed to stare with fascination at what was left of his old friend Tony's kid ... little Tony.

His lip curled, and he said quietly, "Some tiger. The only tiger on this hill, kid, just climbed out that window."

And then the *Capo* went to the liquor cabinet, poured himself a drink, then he sank wearily into a chair and waited for someone to come up and take care of him.

9: WANG DANG DOO

He was two minutes into the hit and the numbers were rapidly running away from him when Bolan dropped to the ground beneath DeMarco's bedroom window.

The smoke at ground level was beginning to dissipate and it was straggling about the neighborhood in puffy clumps.

People were still running about in confusion at the front of the property. Bolan could hear men cursing and shouting inside the house.

Someone in there was yelling, "The fans, get the goddam fans going, blow that shit outta here!"

Another guy leaned out of an upstairs window, coughing and gasping for breathable air. He saw Bolan and took a shot at him, and Bolan quickly responded with a quiet *phu-uut* from the silenced Beretta. The guy gurgled and disappeared back inside. Bolan went on, making tracks across the rear yard and wishing he'd had another thirty seconds of good heavy smoke to cover his withdrawal.

He made it to the garage and was girding himself for the leap to the roof when another man materialized from the thinning smokescreen.

This one was wearing a gas mask with a neat

SFPD emblem on the cannister. He had black hands, and one of these was filled with a snubnosed .38 Positive—and Bolan knew damned well then that he had overrun his numbers.

The guy barked, "Freeze! One move and I'll fire!"

Bolan hesitated for a sluggishly bloated second of solar time, and it was like an eternity in the universe of pure mind. This was the realization of all the Executioner's harshest nightmares—a gun-to-gun and eyeball-to-eyeball confrontation with the law. Cops were special things. Some were rotten, sure, some as rotten as any of the enemy—but they were soldiers on the same side, in Bolan's mind, and that made them special. Mack Bolan did not live to gun down cops.

At the same time and in that same framework of mind, this was no goddam game of touch-tag he was playing. He could not simply roll over and play dead at the first appearance of a dutybound cop. There was a hell of an important war to be fought!

Yeah, it was agonizing. It was a hell of an agonizing real life nightmare.

Sgt. Phillips was realizing with a harsh jolt that neither had the drop on either. He had reacted in pure instinct, with all the training of his adult lifetime focusing into this undiluted moment, this hellishly painful and entirely non-academic moment in the life of a law officer.

The big guy was just standing there, poised in that special way on the balls of his feet, the very mean-looking black Beretta peering up from the gun hand. One side of his consciousness was trying to appreciate the confrontation from a strictly ethereal standpoint, and he actually imagined for one flashing instant that part of him was hovering overhead in a spectator's view of the scene.

Two men, one dressed in black, the other born in black, with a hell of a lot more than the color of skin separating them. One a cop, the other the most wanted "criminal" in the country. Both wearing gasmasks, and each with a trained gun laying down on the other.

And yet there was so goddammed much that these two gladiators shared in common.

The moment came unfrozen, the big guy moved almost imperceptibly, and the Beretta dropped ever so slightly.

"Okay, fire away," Bolan told the law.

"I mean it, Mack. I won't enjoy it, but I'll drop you in your tracks like a Wang Dang Doo."

Gasmasks or not, eight thousand ocean miles and too damn many years between notwithstanding, the message had been sent and received and the Executioner knew his challenger.

The Beretta dropped another inch and the familiar voice said, "Well, damn. Is that you, Bill?"

"That's me." The mask came off but the revolver did not waver. "Don't make me drop you."

Bolan removed his mask and it dropped to the ground. "You might as well," he replied. "I'm a dead man the minute those cuffs go on me anyway."

Phillips felt the flicker of a smile, and he wondered if it had managed to reach the outside of his face. He said, "You hit the old man, eh."

"No. He wasn't the target. It was a tiger hunt."

"I'm going to cuff you, Mack. Throw the gun away and hold that wall up."

The next few seconds occupied a confused kaleidoscope in the mind and the memory of the Brushfire cop.

He certainly was no rookie—and even granted a bit of clumsiness and momentary inattention as he reached for the handcuffs, there was simply no intellectual explanation for the way the big junglefighter turned things upside down on him.

All Phillips knew was that suddenly the Beretta phutted, from the hip, then again and again. All the while Bolan was all over him, manhandling him into a sprawl to the ground, and the Beretta was coughing on in an uninterrupted song of whispering slugs and sighing death.

His own gun was lying at his fingertips and numbly Phillips realized that the zinging little missiles were not tearing into his own flesh, but were seeking more distant game.

Bodies were toppling out there somewhere, in the misty smoke, and the grunts and muffled shrieks of the dying and the grievously wounded served only as a postscript to the booming of opposing weapons as the return fire chewed the turf and whistled screaming tracks in the air above their heads.

The kaleidoscope cleared abruptly. Bill Phillips was back in Vietnam again and his team leader was once again dragging him out of a life and death situation. As he disentangled himself and reclaimed his own weapon, he knew that enemy pursuit had caught them in an open firefight, with a wall at their backs and a regrouped army pressing in from all other sides. Sergeant Bolan was giving 'em hell, throwing everything at them but his own fingers and toes, and giving the rest of the squad a chance to break for cover.

Phillips mumbled, "I'm on you, Sarge."

Bolan grunted, "About time. Watch that left!"

The big silver gun was in Bolan's hand now and the thing was tearing up Phillips' eardrums and totally eclipsing the reports of his own weapon. It served to return him to present time and place, however ... and, really, the situation was little different than it had been so many times before.

Bolan yelled, "Garage roof! Go! You, then me!"

The Brushfire cop reacted instinctively to the command, as he had done to that same voice so many times in the past and with such memorable results. That voice had brought him through Vietnam in one whole piece. He threw a round into a shadowy running figure off to the left, then he flung himself in a wild roll toward the corner of the garage.

Bolan was on one knee and firing the silver hawgleg like an automatic repeater, the big sounds booming, rolling and echoing around the confined area, and guys were still screaming and flopping about out there.

Hot little things zipped through the air about him but Phillips gained the roof in one mad fling, and he found reason to be thankful for all those morning workouts in the police gym. Before his mind even fully appreciated what it was he was trying to accomplish, he was up there at the edge of that roof and throwing a rapid fire into the receding smokescreen, and suddenly Bolan was there beside him and panting, "And a Wang Dang Doo to you too. Let's blow!"

The two ex-partners from another time and another war scrambled to the rear and leaped over the fence into the adjoining grounds.

A moment later they were in good cover and with

104

no visible pursuit from the other side. They lay there for a moment, breathing on each other and chuckling as they'd done so many times before, and presently the cop let out a deep breath and declared, "Well, I damn near got your ass shot up again."

Bolan said, "Do tell."

"If you'd just asked, I could've told you. Rivoli had a stacked deck on you. I mean he had troops all over this damned hill."

"I believe you," Bolan panted. "But I was just about home clean when you jumped in."

"I'm sorry, Mack. They brainwash you in those police academies. A guy gets all hung up on—"

"Forget it. You're right and I'm wrong. Hell, I'm as wrong as a guy ever got."

"Not quite," the cop reminded him. "You didn't throw down on me, brother." He laughed nervously. "Although, for a minute there, Sergeant, I sure thought you had."

Bolan was breathing raggedly through his mouth and forcing some big ornery-looking bullets into the clip of the silver hawgleg. "You'll have to take me in dead, Bill," he declared quietly.

"Shit I'm not taking you anywhere," Phillips replied. "My gun's empty and I guess I'm at your mercy."

Bolan chuckled.

The Sergeant said, "Did you know that Gadgets Schwartz and the Politician are living here now?"

Bolan's head snapped to attention and he asked, "In San Francisco?"

"Yeah. You haven't been in touch, eh?"

"Hell no. Last thing in the world those guys need now is my touch of death. They holed up?"

"In a manner of speaking, yeah. They've got new names. Gadgets is doing electronics work for a guy down on the marina. Politician is doing something at the Boy's Club. He was always good with kids, you know."

Bolan said, "Yeah." He sighed. "They okay?"

"Yeah, they're great. Worry about *you* a lot. Keep track of your *banzai* war, you know."

"They have any money problems?"

"Not that I know about."

Bolan gave his old friend the cold stare and asked him, "You keeping track of my war, Bill?"

The cop said, "Sure."

"It was no accident that you showed up at DeMarco's."

"Course not. I've been sitting there waiting for you to show since three o'clock this morning."

Bolan grinned suddenly and said, "You're the spade cop out at the gate awhile ago."

Phillips showed him a baffled smile. "Where were you?"

"I was around. So . . . you came gunning for me."

The Sergeant dropped his eyes in embarrassment. He changed the subject. "Hell, I can't get used to looking at that face, Mack. What was wrong with the old one?"

Bolan shrugged. "Seemed like a good idea at the time. I guess it doesn't matter which face I'm buried with."

The dark face of the law clouded with an unhappy thought as Phillips said, "This is just a temporary truce, Mack. We'll probably meet again, if you ever come back to San Francisco. And I can't . . . I mean, you know. So don't come back."

106

Bolan reminded him, "I haven't left yet. I'll be around awhile."

"God, don't. Get out. Blow this town, man. It's hot. Captain Matchison wants your ass with a burning passion."

"Brushfire," Bolan commented thoughtfully.

"How'd you know?"

"I hear. Are you with Brushfire, Bill?"

"Yeah."

Bolan said, "Well, good luck. Everything okay with your life?"

"Until today, yeah."

"These tough Frisco cops didn't give you a hard time?"

The black man snorted, "Hell, I'm a tough Frisco cop myself."

Bolan agreed, "That you are." He got to his feet, squeezed the other man's shoulder affectionately, and told him, "Blow, cop, before we get into another Wang Dang Doo."

They shook hands and Phillips said, "That was a hell of a place, wasn't it."

"It was," Bolan agreed.

"So is this place, Mack. It's Wang Dang Doo times ten. Believe that."

A muscle rippled in the Executioner's jaw and he replied, "I believe it."

"Get out."

"I can't."

"The mission that important?"

Bolan sighed. "I think so."

"End of truce," the cop said. "Goodbye, soldier. Next time we meet, it's Wang Dang Doo." He glanced at his watch. "You might still have about thirty seconds to beat the grid. That's what we call the containment network. Thirty seconds, if you're lucky."

He turned his back and walked away.

Bolan faded quietly into the opposite direction.

Every second counted now. And he wasn't about to scrub this mission even if it was Wang Dang Doo times a thousand.

It was, yeah, a damned important mission.

10: ABLE TEAM

Wang Dang Doo, and Hanoi too.

It had been one of those private jokes of a handful of scared-out-of-their-skull warriors known as Penetration Team Able. Bolan was the ranking non-com, the team leader. The entire team actually existed as a tactical support unit for the special skills of their leader—Executioner Bolan.

Maybe there really was a Wang Dang Doo somewhere, Bolan never knew. Some of the places they hit over there didn't have a name. Some didn't even have a permanent geographical existence. The enemy in Vietnam had been a highly mobile force. Sometimes Able Team had been required to track a Charlie command post halfway across the deltas before they could set up a strike.

Under Bolan, Able Team had ranged up and down the Ho Chi Minh trail. They'd made a few quiet excursions through the DMZ and into the strongholds of the Northmen. Several times they'd found themselves tracking deep into Laos or Cambodia.

There had been no sanctuaries from Able Team. And none, incidentally, *for* them when they were on a mission.

There had been dozens of Wang Dang Doos. The

term, reduced to its utter simplicity, simply meant a rub-out. A wipe-out. A slaughter.

That had been Bolan's specialty.

Sniper, yes. Stiletto man, yes. Garroter, bone-crusher, spine-cracker—yes, all of these were in Bolan's bag of tricks. And he had not been the only specialist in Vietnam. But for the specialty of specialties, Able Team was always the pick of the list. They always got the gory ones. And they got the tough ones because they did the job better.

Able Team had *the Executioner*.

This was not an item of pride for Mack Bolan. He accepted the medals, the decorations, the special scrolls from grateful villages—but he put them quietly away in a box and forgot them.

Killing people had never meant anything more to Bolan than a distasteful chore which had to be done. He recognized the fact that he had developed a high proficiency in the art of killing, and he recognized also that this proficiency obligated him to a special responsibility. A war needed winning—or, at least, it needed to be contained and controlled. Bolan had the tools, the abilities, and the toughness of soul required for the proper discharge of particularly grisly responsibilities.

He recognized this, but he had taken no special pride in that recognition.

Wang Dang Doo, and Hanoi too.

Yeah, there had been a lot of Bills and Bobs and Toms and Dicks. Kids, most of them, scared out of their skulls—forever wondering why they'd volunteered for this hellfire team. At least Bolan had Korea behind him. He hadn't come into the war with story-book ideas of what it was all about.

Bill Phillips was not the first of the PenTeam graduates Bolan had run into during this new war. He'd even thought once that he could pull together an American civilian version of the old death squads, and he'd actually pulled one together ... briefly. The results were tragic; enough so to convince Bolan that it could never work over here.

Herman "Gadgets" Schwartz and Rosario "Politician" Blancanales were the sole survivors of that experiment. They'd squared their account with the law, but they'd have the mob on their asses forever—that much was certain. They were marked men ... marked for death.

No more. Not ever again. Bolan would never involve another human being in his private war, not as an ally.

This was a specialty war. A Wang Dang Doo in the real sense, and a job for a loner, without support, a guy who knew every way and every wile, a guy who could stride through rivers of blood to kill again and again ... and be willing to take his lumps in that final judgement of the universe.

Yeah. And there it was, of course. Mack Bolan was not a religious man. Not in the ordinary sense of praying and going to church and that sort of thing. But he knew that the universe did not run itself. It wasn't a damn machine which just suddenly sprang into being and then began running down. There was a purpose to the whole thing ... somewhere beyond the fragmented understanding of ordinary mortals there was a good reason for the existence of the universe.

If feeling one's self a contributing particle of that

111

universe could be regarded as a religion, then Bolan was a religious man.

In this world of order and purpose, a self-aware particle called Mack Bolan had received some manner of special endowments. He had developed skills, and he had grown into a uniqueness of personal destiny which somehow seemed to have some importance.

Yes, this was a hell of an important mission.

Bolan's war with the Mafia was of some definite importance to the universal order of things.

He was obligated to an exercise of a special responsibility.

He was a Wang Dang Doo type of guy, face it, and he could turn away from his responsibilities no more than he could turn away from life itself.

And, in this hot old town of San Francisco, the star performer of Able Team had again drawn the tough one, the gory one.

This time it would be *Wang Dang Doo, and Mr. King too.*

And there would be no sanctuaries—neither of geography, nor of social rank, nor of family background—there would be no sanctuaries from this Wang Dang Doo.

The Executioner was tracking the hit.

11: DETENTE

The decals were off and the warwagon was slowly cruising the periphery of the DeMarco neighborhood.

Bolan knew something about containment networks; he himself had set up one or two in years gone by—and there were certain telltale signs a savvy prey could look for ... to give him that extra few seconds of pre-reaction before he found himself bouncing off the net.

The idea was to avoid touching the net. It was like a spring trap ... one touch and you're caught.

Bolan had re-assumed his role camouflage, this time with a blue denim jacket instead of the white windbreaker and lightly tinted purple lenses over the eyes in lieu of the bushy mustache. The effect was about the same—a subtle shift of image that wasn't overly noticeable, not clown-like, simply innocuous. A busy wad of chewing gum kept his jaws in wobbling motion, adding a further distortion to the basic image.

He was about three blocks from the DeMarco mansion when he spotted the first trap car. It was parked at the curb on the corner of Hyde and Pacific, an ordinary street cruiser with engine idling, two uniformed men in front and two plainclothesmen in the rear. The barrel of a sawed-off shotgun was visible

113

above the back seat and a teargas gun lay on the rear deck.

One block beyond that was a neatly concealed roadblock. They were making it look like a minor traffic mishap, with two cars pulled together in a T-formation just outside the intersection, a wrecker visible in the background, one narrow lane of traffic open and being slowly moved along by a uniformed officer.

Most vehicles would be passed on through without too much delay. Certain ones would be maneuvered through the block and into a special "inspection pool" immediately beyond the set-up ... probably over behind the wrecker. It was cute, very cute, and once a guy committed himself to that scene there would be no way out.

Bolan was not about to commit himself.

He pulled alongside the plug cruiser and stopped, then slid across the seat and rolled down the window. He said, "Hey man," and popped his gum at the guy.

The uniformed cop at the wheel of the cruiser gave him a scowl and nothing else.

Bolan scowled back and asked him, "What happened to Lombard? It was right here yesterday."

The cop growled, "Beat it."

"Don't freak out, man. I just want to know where Lombard Street is."

"Get that crate out of here, you're blocking our view."

"Well you could at least—"

"Go ask a service station! Move on, right now!"

Bolan said, "Amen man." He blew a bubble with the gum, casually raised the window, slid back behind the wheel, and sent the van creaking around the corner and away from the blockade.

His recently abandoned "drop"—the old apartment building—was two short blocks dead ahead. Under the circumstances, the apartment now seemed to represent the lesser of two possible evils. Obviously he had not "beat the grid"—and, just as obviously, he would not do so in any sort of running play. That hill was crawling with cops equipped with cute games and full riot gear.

One of the more important strategies of warfare was in knowing when to use your weapons, when to use your feet, and when to use your tail. Right now seemed an appropriate occasion to use the tail.

Bolan parked the warwagon a half-block from his building, locked it securely, and went the rest of the way on foot. He used the front entrance and the regular stairway, and he arrived at his own door on the third floor without incident.

The smell of fresh coffee struck him as he pushed into the apartment. The Beretta met his hand halfway and led him around the corner into the kitchen.

The China doll, wearing the same clothing and an entirely unsurprised smile, glanced at the Beretta Belle and cheerily announced, "Coffee's ready."

"It was ready hours ago," he reminded her.

"I threw that out. This is new."

Bolan went on past her and shook the place down. It was clean. He returned to the entrance hall and closed the door, then he went into the living room to gaze glumly out the window. The police had finally closed on the DeMarco place, and blue uniforms were moving vigorously all around those distant grounds.

115

The girl came up behind him and carefully halted several paces to the rear. She asked him, "Were those your fireworks I heard awhile ago?"

He returned the Beretta to the sideleather, dropped tiredly into an overstuffed chair, and told the China doll, "Yeah. Special celebration, no charge to spectators."

In a small voice she informed him, "I came in through the window."

Bolan said, "Great. You can go out the same way."

Instead she went into the kitchen and returned a moment later with two steaming mugs of coffee. "How do you take it?" she asked.

"Strong, black, and not drugged."

She laughed and pushed a mug at him. "You've seen too many movies."

He accepted the coffee. "I haven't seen a movie in four years."

She wrinkled her nose and sat down opposite him, daintily holding the oversized mug with both hands. "You haven't missed much. Skin is in, drama is out, comedy is sick, and sick is relevant."

Bolan chuckled. He put down the coffee to light a cigarette, savored the invigorating smoke briefly, and expelled it in a tired whoosh. Then he asked the girl, "Why'd you come back?"

"Wrong question," she replied solemnly.

"What's the right one?"

"Why did I leave."

"Okay, why did you?"

She tossed her head and said, "Give me one of those damn cigarettes."

He tossed her the pack, then leaned forward to light her. When they had both settled down again, the

116

China doll said, "I'll bet you never would have asked, would you."

He shrugged. "You had a right. It's your neck."

"I didn't leave because of my neck," she told him.

"No?"

"No." She sipped the coffee and worked at the cigarette for another long moment, then: "*Your* neck."

"Tell me about it."

"Mr. Wo Fan, I fear, is a dirty rat."

"Why didn't you fear that when you introduced us?"

"Because I. . . ."

"What?"

She was busying her speech equipment with a delicate and thoughtful sipping at the coffee cup. Bolan stood up and removed the denim jacket. He put the purple lenses in a pocket of the jacket and came out of his gunleather.

The Auto Mag was locked up in the warwagon. The Beretta Belle he deposited on a table at his right hand, then he slipped off the Levi bluejeans and dropped them to the floor with the jacket. The blacksuit smelled faintly of gunpowder and blood.

Bolan rubbed at a large stain on his sleeve and returned to the chair with a sigh.

Mary Ching was giving him the unblinking appraisal. In a quiet voice she told him, "I like you better that way. You look like just what you are."

"And what is that?"

"A death machine."

He curtly nodded his head and told her, "Okay, I accept that."

"And the very image of male virility."

He said, "I'll accept that too."

117

She smiled, almost timidly. "Right now?"

He replied, "Hell no, not right now."

She giggled.

Gruffly he said, "Watch it. I've already killed a couple million people this morning."

"You can joke about it?" she asked soberly.

Bolan sighed and told her, "It beats crying about it."

"It does bother you, then?"

"Sure it bothers me. Wouldn't it bother you?"

She blinked her eyes. "I don't know. I guess it would depend on who I was killing."

"It doesn't matter *who*, dead is dead," he said.

"You're a weird hombre, Mr. Executioner," the girl informed him. "I guess that's why I left, and it's why I came back."

"Because I'm weird."

"Right."

"Okay."

"You don't ask many questions, do you."

He said, "Only when they seem important."

She stared at the tip of her cigarette and seemed to be talking to it instead of Bolan. "I left because I don't deserve your protection. And I came back because you do deserve mine."

He threw it back at her. "Thanks, but I guess I don't want it."

She appeared to be a bit confused. "You'd let me just walk out of here, I mean right now?"

"Sure, if you want to."

"Then you trust me?"

"No I do not."

The China doll chewed on her lower lip and crushed out the cigarette in an ashtray in a slow and deliberate mauling of the tobacco. "You're a very frustrating conversationalist," she told him.

Why not? That perplexing little chunk of Oriental beauty had crawled right back into his guts again, and it wasn't a nice feeling.

In a voice very tired but firm he told her, "Hell, Mary, I haven't slept for about thirty hours. I haven't eaten for sixteen. I've made two very hard hits on this town and I've killed a hell of a lot of people. Now I wasn't worrying about any of this until you walked out of here a couple of hours ago. Don't ask me why, it just bugged me suddenly and I had to puke the whole mess up. And I was okay again until I walked in here and smelled your damned coffee. So what do you want of me? What the hell do you want?"

She licked her lip and said, "Wow, you *can* talk."

He muttered, "Go to hell."

"What are you planning on doing now?"

"Nothing."

"I mean. . . ."

"I'm sewed in. Cops all over the place. So I'm going to get some sleep."

"Oh. Well that's perfectly clear, I guess. The cops are all around, so you're just going to crawl peacefully into bed and catch a few winks."

"That's exactly right."

"You're weird, Mack Bolan. You're really weird. Why don't you pace the floor, like the caged rats do in the movies. Why don't you get drunk or beat me up or something. Why don't you go over and smash out the window, stick your gun outside and scream out your defiance to a world that's laying all over you."

Bolan laughed, and it felt good. He did not feel like

119

puking anything up now. He told the girl, "You're something else."

"I haven't had much sleep either," she solemnly reminded him.

"Be my guest," he said, as solemnly.

"Okay. Have you ever had a Chinese bath?"

He thought it over briefly, then replied, "I guess not."

"I'll give you one."

He said, "Okay."

"Don't you start one-wording me again."

"You've got enough for both of us," he told her.

She said, "Weird. This is really weird. I don't believe it. This is the weirdest seduction scene I've ever been in."

He chuckled and asked her, "Who's seducing whom?"

She said, "If you don't know, we're both in trouble."

The two of them left the room clinging to each other and laughing, and Bolan was feeling better than he had for some time.

It wasn't so bad to have to stand alone. That wasn't the worst part. What really got to a guy after awhile was *lying* alone. Genuine human companionship could be a rare thing in a war zone, especially for a one man army.

For awhile, for a very brief period of détente, the Executioner would find some exquisite human companionship. Perhaps it would have to be enough to last him a lifetime. An hour, a day, perhaps even a week. Yeah, a lifetime.

12: COUNTERATTACK, TIMES TWO

Captain Matchison was in a steel-chewing mood and Sgt. Bill Phillips was feeling more the rookie than at any time in his career.

They were in the Brushfire mobile command post, and all of the detail leaders had been called in for an ass-chewing.

Bill Phillips was a detail leader.

It had been his job to pin the tail on the cat and he'd ended up with it pinned to himself.

It was bad enough to be black in a white man's world. It was plain miserable to be both black and incompetent. He'd had to tell the Captain the full story. What the hell. It was no time to be cute with your lord god.

Matchison was standing at the side window, glaring at the mess in the DeMarco yard. One balled fist was slowly beating out a controlled rhythm on the glass. The other hand was shoved deep into his pants pocket. The guy never showed much expression in the face. He didn't need to. Forcefields of anger radiated away from him like a satanic halo whenever he was feeling this way. A mad scowl or a cutting word would seem almost like a pat on the back at a time like this.

The other sergeants were semi-circled behind Phillips. He could not see them but he could feel them could sense their embarrassment and frustration. This was an uptight outfit. They had to be. Theirs was an uptight business. They were the elite in the town of the elite, and they had to prove it with every job that came up.

Matchison broke a two minute silence with, "I don't believe it."

Phillips said, "Captain, I—"

"Shut up, Sergeant Phillips," lord god commanded. "Don't remind me of your temporary insanity. I was just counting the stretchers out there. Do you know how many I've counted so far?"

"I guess a few," the Sergeant muttered.

"Try seventeen, and that's just for openers. The meds are still rounding them up and packing them out."

"Yessir, it was a hard hit."

"How many of those bodies do you figure are yours?"

The Sergeant wondered if he could safely light a cigarette. He decided not, and told the Captain, "No more than one or two, I'd say. The PM will tell. I use a .38 Positive. Mack had—the suspect was using two different weapons. One was a foreign job, not too heavy, probably a nine millimeter. Had a silencer on it. The other pistol was—hell I don't know what it was. I'd never seen anything like it."

"What do you mean?"

"I mean I'd never seen a gun like that before. About a foot long, looked like stainless steel. Hooded barrel with ventilators. I watched him refill the clip. I'd never seen bullets like those, either."

"Hand loads, maybe?"

"Probably, yes, sir. The guy is a gunsmith. Maybe he even made the gun."

"I'll want that in a written report," the Captain snapped.

"Yessir."

Matchison swung away from the window to directly confront his black cop with a hard and level stare. "Bill . . . I'm going to try to cover you this time."

"Thanks, I appreciate it," Phillips murmured.

"But I want that GI buddy of yours!"

"Yessir, I know that."

"You stay away from him!"

"Sir?"

"I don't want anybody screaming around town that the department is cooperating in a mob wipe-out!"

"Captain, I wasn't in on the hit with him, I just got caught in the crossfire, and Bolan pulled my ass out of there for me. That's all."

Matchison's eyes rolled and he said, "Not a word of that had better get in the press. Understand?"

"Yessir," Phillips replied miserably.

"Caen or one of those guys gets ahold of a story like that and the town will laugh us across the Golden Gate."

"Bolan saved my life," the Sergeant muttered.

"That's exactly what I mean! Now just look at the thing, Bill. Look at it from an outside viewpoint. We're on a full Brushfire alert. We have the town nailed down tight and just waiting for the guy to show. The powerful Brushfire Force, your city's answer to rampant crime in the streets, the elite squad of our police department—all of these great, highly trained, highly paid police officers—against one lonely

123

and desperate man. And so what happens. The guy casually drops in through one of our stakeouts, rubs out at least seventeen of our citizens who are not—*not*, remember—under indictment for any crimes—and then not only gets away clean but hangs around long enough to *rescue* one of our officers. Now, Bill ... I want *that* God damned story to die right here in this vehicle."

"It's dead," Phillips assured his Captain.

One of the detail leaders behind him asked, "Is the smoking lamp lit, Captain?"

"Yeah, smoke, why not," Matchison growled. "Get comfortable, all of you. Get very comfortable for about ten minutes, because it's the last comfort you're going to find for quite awhile."

Bill Phillips believed it. He sank wearily onto a canvas chair and lit a cigarette, then sat there for considerably more than ten minutes listening to Captain Matchison's plans for Mack Bolan.

And when he left that command post with the other detail leaders, Phillips knew that it was a whale of a plan. Not even Mack Bolan, the soldier of the century, would find a loophole of comfort in the determined strategy of Jim Matchison.

And the Wang Dang kid from Able Team knew a terrible and penetrating sadness. Somewhere out there in that city the greatest human being he'd ever known was going to be run-to-ground, and impaled upon the horns of *quote* justice *unquote*, or else shot down in the streets like some sort of runaway beast.

It was a hell of a way to run a world, but that was the way the world ran ... the only way.

Guys like Mack Bolan didn't stand a chance.

But ... and this was the most terrible part ... what

124

chance did the world itself stand?—*without* guys like Mack Bolan.

Bill Phillips was a cop, sure.

He was a tough San Francisco Brushfire cop.

But there were times when he wished to God he *wasn't*.

He was going to kill Mack Bolan. It was his right, his obligation, and he owed it. He owed it to Mack Bolan.

Able Team would do the job better.

From one of Union Square's more expensive hotel suites, another kind of army was being ordered into the field. The suite "at the top of the joint" represented the fulfillment of a lifelong ambition for "Crazy Franco" Laurentis, the torpedo's torpedo and boss of the silk suit brigade.

"Style," Laurentis enjoyed telling anyone who would listen, "is the only thing makes life worthwhile. A man should live in style. He should eat, dress and screw in style, he even ought to die in style. I'd live in this joint if it took every cent I made just to keep me here."

It took quite a bit. The five room penthouse apartment provided one of the most breathtaking views in a city made famous by its views. From the garden terrace, from the glass-walled living room, or from just about any window in that joint, this silk-suited graduate of such institutions as Sing Sing, Leavenworth and Folsom could gaze out over the toughest town in the west and experience the giddy feeling of domain and lordship. One day he would be commanding that town, he would be holding it in his hands just as surely as he now held it in his vision—and he'd do it all from right here, from the top of the joint—because Franco Laurentis *was the tops*.

Let Vanity Vince and Tom the Broker have their pipedreams—it was all they would have. With or without old man DeMarco, Franco Laurentis was by God going to have San Francisco.

A death, a simple death, that's all it took. A seventy-two year old man was not going to go on living forever. Death was cheap, of course. It was the cheapest thing going. Franco could buy any life in that town for less than it cost him to live at the top of the joint for a week.

A hit on a *Capo*, of course, could be a messy business. There would be the eastern coalition of commissioners to explain things to, and they sometimes got their asses high in the air over a hit on a *Capo*. Even an old, already dying, *Capo* like Roman DeMarco. Even though Roman had never been too popular in life, his death would bring on a lot of tears and sympathy from the eastern mob.

Franco didn't need any of that.

It was easier to do the thing in style, to just let the old man die his own way, and meanwhile Franco could go on quietly pulling the loose ends together so it would be an easy slide from the wake to the throne.

Sometimes, of course, *style* took a lot of patience. The old man acted like he wanted to go on living forever. Some guys just never knew when to throw in the towel. So Franco had been very patiently unravelling the goddam towel and throwing it in *for* him, a thread at a time, and of course he was throwing those threads right into his own pocket.

Franco was not even in the official line of succession. Tom Vericci was first man out, by right of business power and seniority if nothing else. Vince Ciprio was running a close second. Franco wasn't even in the running. If Tom moved up to fill the old man's dead shoes, he'd move some one of his lieutenants right up to fill *his* vacated shoes. Ciprio would stand still. Franco would stand still. And, worst of all, he'd have to work under the thumb of Tom the Broker. Bullshit, buddy!

Vince, of course, would like to be at the head of the line. But Vince just didn't have the style to be a *Capo*. Tom, now—Tom the Broker was a hell of a classy guy. Deep down in his bowels, Crazy Franco was a little afraid of Tom Vericci. But not so damned afraid that he wouldn't contract the guy, if it got to that.

Franco Laurentis had the torpedo concession in this town.

Nobody, *by God*, had better not ever forget that.

Especially Vanity Vince and Tom the Broker.

He could take them both out with a nod of his head, if it got to that. That would make a war, of course. And the eastern coalition got nervous over open wars. It hurt the whole outfit, really. Franco understood that. That's why he continued to work with style.

It would be so much better to just have this understanding, before things ever got to open war.

And Franco was about to weld that understanding into the minds of all who wanted to operate in this town.

Mack the Bastard had come to town . . . and hell, it had come like a gift from the angels or something.

Some very stylish use could be made of Mack the Bastard. The guy liked to go for the *Capos*—that was why the organization was so nervous all over the country. They wouldn't be that nervous if the guy was just knocking over a few soldiers here and there. Soldiers were cheap, and soldiers didn't have a hell of a lot to say about how nervous the organization got. It got nervous as hell, though, when the big boys were in trouble. Franco could appreciate that point of view. He was a big boy himself, now. And he was going to get bigger.

Bolan was going to knock over *Don* DeMarco. That was a pre-ordained fact of life, and Franco knew it. He knew it because he didn't intend to do a damned little thing to stop the guy. For God's sake, why should he?

The time for doing something would come later. Later, after the old man was totally out of the picture. And in the meantime Franco would be in undisputed charge of the town. He was already ... practically ... in every way that counted. He had the whole town, right in his hands. The dumb bastards Ciprio and Vericci had just handed it over to him. *Take* it, *take* it. So he took it, damn right.

Those guys were in for one hell of a shock if they thought he was just going to hand it all back after Bolan was out of the way.

After all, the guy that took out Mack the Bastard deserved some recognition, didn't he? Franco would be the hero of the outfit, all over the world. And Franco's stock would be that much higher when things finally came to the showdown with Ciprio and Vericci. No one would yell too much or too loud at the guy who finally got Bolan—not even the coalition back east. Especially if that guy was already Franco Laurentis.

Thus had been the reasoning of the stylish torpedo from the top of the joint—until approximately eight thirty on that morning of the California Hit. It was at about that time when *Don* DeMarco himself telephoned Franco to rake him over the coals in a most humiliating and unstylish way.

"You son of a bitch you!" the old man screamed at him. "I give you a special job and what do you do with it? You take it to bed and sleep with it? In that rich cunt-castle of yours up in the sky? Huh?"

That wasn't no way to be talking to the Lord Enforcer of San Francisco, even if the speaker was the *Capo*, and the tone of voice—more than the words themselves—sent a cold tremor through Franco's belly.

"Wh-what's the matter?" he stammered. "Wh-what're you talking about?"

"I'm-a talk-about-a this-a Bolan-a bastard," the old man screamed, lapsing into a heavy accent in his rage. "He come in here and knocked my place over! He hit Tony's kid and twenty or thirty other boys! He shot up my place and missed hitting me by an eyelash! Whatta you think I'm-a talk about, you dumb Dago torpedo, what the hell you think I talk about? Why you not onna street, why you not out there chasin' this boy's a-head all over town, huh?"

Franco Laurentis was not no dumb Dago torpedo. But it hardly seemed the appropriate time to be arguing the point.

Faintly, he said, "God, that's awful, *Don* DeMarco. He got away clean? He didn't even leave any blood?"

"He left a God damn-a *medal*, that's-a what! You get your ass onna streets, Franco! Get down outta that ivory cunt tower and start doin' something *right* for a change!"

129

"I got everything moving, sir," Laurentis tried to assure the boss. "I guarantee you, we're gonna have that boy before the sun sets again."

"You sure about that, huh?"

"Yes sir, I am sure, I am positive sure about that."

"You better be. I'm-a tell-a you why you better be. I named you in my will, Franco."

"I don't, uh, I guess I don't get you," Laurentis told *Capo*.

"You gonna die *with* me, Franco!"

"What—I don't—you mean. . . ?"

"You know what I mean! I got your name on five pieces of paper. *Five* pieces, Franco. If I die by Bolan, you die by the paper! You better keep that in mind!"

The old bastard! He'd *contracted* Franco Laurentis!

He said, "I don't think that's . . . I mean, I think I got a right to discuss this with you."

"You got no rights! I give you a job! You do the job! You damn sure better do the job, Franco!"

And that was it. The nutty old bastard hung up on him.

And a whole new style of thinking and acting had suddenly entered Franco's life. If he had just *known* which five were holding those pieces of paper. Hell, it could be anybody. They could be from back East, they could be from anywhere in the damn world! But he *didn't* know, and there wasn't time enough left to track them down. *They* would be tracking *Franco* down the minute the old man bit Bolan's dust. *God!* An *estate* contract!

Ten minutes after the conclusion of that telephone conversation, Franco Laurentis, the torpedo's torpedo, was conducting a full scale council of war at the top

130

of the joint. He had all his boys in there, and there wouldn't be any shitting around with style now.

The sly old fox was not dead yet, and he'd sure put it over on Franco. That was something that just had to be faced. It was a new game.

There was only one thing for Franco to do now.

He had to stop Mack Bolan before Mack Bolan stopped the old man.

There was nothing else he could do.

He would have to turn in Bolan's head, or else die without no damn style at all.

The torpedo's torpedo was *not* going to die without no damn style at all.

13: THE ALLIANCE

The gunleather was strapped to the side-railing of the bed and Bolan's hand was resting loosely on the grip of the Beretta Belle.

Another hand, a softly delicate one, was trying to come between Bolan and his Belle.

He opened an eye halfway and quietly commanded, "Don't."

She was lying partly across him, the velvety tenderness of her presenting the sweetest of burdens, one arm coiled down around his gun arm.

She whispered, "I thought you were asleep."

He told her, "I was."

"Well, that's some alarm system you've got there."

She moved away from him. The bedsprings creaked as she came to a kneeling position behind him.

Bolan voluntarily released the Beretta, as he rolled over to fix her in the binocular vision of both appreciative eyes.

"Do you always sleep with a hand on your gun?" she asked him.

"Until I get tired of living, sure."

"I'm sorry. I didn't understand. I just didn't want you going into a bad dream or something and shooting up the joint."

132

He said, "Okay."

"You really don't trust me, do you."

He said, "No."

"Even after . . ."

"Especially after," he told her.

Her eyes crossed in perplexity. "Boy, you sure live in a grim world, don't you."

"Like you said, I'm weird."

She wrinkled her nose and replied, "Sort of *nice* weird, though. Mack . . . are you wide awake?"

He assured her that he was.

She said, "I want to bare my chest."

Bolan grinned. "I like it just the way it is," he told her.

"You know what I mean. I want to get straight with you. No more mistrust. Okay?"

He said, "Suit yourself."

"Wouldn't you *like* to trust me?"

He tipped his head back and said, "Sure I would."

"Well listen to me. Wo Fan and Franco Laurentis are hooked together somehow."

Bolan's eyes flickered and he said, "Do tell."

"You already knew it, huh."

"I've been wondering."

"Well you can stop wondering. They definitely are. It's one of those marriages of convenience, I believe, but they definitely—"

"And the old cop?"

"Barney Gibson?"

He said, "Uh huh."

"Do I have to get that bare?"

He said, "No."

The girl sighed. "Well, I will. I have been in the employ of Barney Gibson."

"Who else have you been in the employ of?"

Her gaze fell. "Anyone who has the price, I guess," she admitted.

"And what is the price?"

She said, "Depends on the job."

"What is the nature of the work?"

"Intelligence."

Both eyes narrowed as Bolan asked her, "You telling me you're a private eye?"

She threw her head back and laughed, as though grateful for the break. "Not really. I'm not licensed." The eyes flashed wickedly and she added, "But I have a law degree and I once worked for Mr. Hoover."

Bolan groaned.

She asked him, "You have something against Mr. Hoover?"

He replied, "Just his womenfolk. I think women's lib must have pulled a secret coup on the federal level. Do you know how many federal dolls I've—"

Quickly she said, "I don't want to know, don't tell me. Anyway, I said I *once* worked for him. I've been freelancing for two years."

"Without license."

"Right, without license. I'm not public. A license would hamper me. I'm not a detective, Mack. I'm a spy."

He said, "Okay. What's the tie-in with Barney Gibson then? He paying you out of his own pocket?"

"Possibly. I wouldn't know if the city has a payroll code for paid informers."

He said, "I see."

"I've also been on Wo Fan's payroll, watching the operation at China Gardens."

"For what?"

"I don't know for what. I just watch and listen. Every night I file a written report of everything I've seen and heard."

"That business about the counterfeit art pieces . . . ?"

She wrinkled her face and admitted, "I made that up."

The girl leaned forward suddenly and kissed him, lightly. It turned into a heavy one, and she pulled away gasping.

"Don't get me started again," she warned.

Bolan chuckled. He lightly caressed a silken arm and told her, "I don't have to trust you, Mary. I like you, and that's enough for now."

"Not for me," she said soberly. "What about instincts? Don't they count for anything? Can't you just *know* that I'm on your side now?"

He arched an eyebrow and said, "Now?"

She shrugged delicately. "I'm straighting it, I'll straight it all the way. I suspected that Wo Fan had an unholy interest in the Mafia even before I ran into you. Franco Laurentis tried to grab me by the rear one night. When I told him to get lost, he got real cute about our 'common interests' and he actually dropped Wo Fan's name on me. I mentioned the incident to Wo Fan the next day. He became very upset and started throwing out excited instructions, in Chinese, to his bully boys. I didn't know what he was saying, but—"

"You don't *kapish* Chinese?"

She smiled tolerantly. "Do you kapish Polish?"

He grinned back. "No. How'd you know about my Polack background?"

She told him, "I know a lot of things about you, Mack Bolan. Or I thought I did, until this morning. Anyway . . . the next time I ran into Franco Laurentis—it was a couple of nights later—he came over and made it a point to apologize to me for his behavior. Which, if you know anything about *that* dude, you'll know is way out of character. But he was using the apology as a cover up. His real purpose was to make me think he'd been kidding about Wo Fan. About 'common interests,' I mean."

Bolan said, "Okay, I see it."

"So . . . anyway . . . when I ran into you at the Gardens last night, I . . . . Well, I'm a working girl, you know." She gave him a rueful smile. "Have to pay the damn bills, you know. I guess I . . . had you in about the same running class as Laurentis and the rest. I mean. . . ."

"I know what you mean," Bolan assured her, sighing.

"I knew that you'd been billed as the all-American folk hero, but I figured . . . well, you know what I figured. I know what these public relations people can do with an image, and the press is no different. I had you figured as a glory guy. You know. Soldier-of-fortune type, making a big name and a big game for yourself by running around making big noises at the mob."

"I know what you mean," he assured her.

"Will you please let me bare myself in my own way?"

He chuckled. "Right on."

"Well then I came into this . . . *this* place." She

shivered. "I saw how you ... how you had to make it. I mean, the super security, the constant *grinding* race to just keep that one step ahead of the world. Oh hell, Mack Bolan, I felt so miserable for you, I could have just cried!"

Bolan told her, "Hey, it's not all that bad."

She said, "The hell it's not. I know better. I know it now. And I almost ... I almost set you up for them. Did you know that? I came within an inch of setting you up for Franco's assassins."

"What makes you think they weren't after *you*?"

"Well I. ..."

He said, "They wouldn't have come after me that way, Mary. I never have thought that they expected to find *me* there. That was supposed to be an easy hit, girl. Why do you think I insisted on dragging you out of there?"

She shivered again and said, "Well—damn, *damn*. Sure, Laurentis started worrying about his slip to me. I'll bet you're right."

He said, "Sure I am. And then you threw it back at me. Bugged out. I figured you as good as dead. Maybe that's why I. ..."

"Why you what?"

"Never mind. Why did you leave, Mary?"

"Conscience, I guess. Suddenly I just couldn't stand myself."

Bolan could appreciate that.

"I mean," she went on, "I just had to get out of here. I went back to my place, hoping that Captain couldn't locate Wo Fan anywhere. Then I got to thinking about Cynthie and Panda, and it worried me sick."

"What did?"

"The fact that they had seen you at my place.

Listen, Mack. Those girls work for Wo Fan. Indirectly, but they do. And they know it. It's part of the convenient marriage I mentioned. Wo Fan and Laurentis are entertwined in several ventures in this town. And I got to thinking. ..."

"Yeah," he prompted her.

"If they started talking it around about seeing you there. ... At *my* place. And Laurentis knew about my connections with Wo Fan. And if Wo Fan didn't want Laurentis to know that he was trying to arrange another marriage, with *you*. And if—"

Bolan was laughing.

"What's so funny?"

"Not funny," he said, "just entertaining. It's nice to watch a China doll's mind busily whirring out a web of intrigue. But I think you're probably right."

She jerked her head in an adamant affirmation. "Darned right I am, and those two empty kids could be in a whole lot of trouble."

"Yes, they could," Bolan mused. "I warned them to keep quiet. But they probably won't."

She agreed. "Anyway, I tried to find them. I called everywhere I thought they could have gone."

Bolan said, "She mentioned something about a houseboat. In Sausalito, I believe."

"They wouldn't have gone over there. They're shooting a picture. It's too hard for them to run back and forth when they're shooting. They crash around town all the time they're shooting."

"How'd you get mixed up with those kids, Mary?"

She sniffed. "They're not as bad as they talk it. Panda is pretty mixed up, about sex and what her's is, I mean, but ... well, they're okay kids. I met them

138

through Wo Fan, at a business bash he was hosting a few months ago. They were, uh, paid guests."

Bolan said, "I see."

"*I* was *not*."

He chuckled. "Where do you go from here, Mary?"

"Into the woodwork, I guess. How about you?"

A faint smile pulled at his lips. He said, "I've got this war."

She wrinkled her nose at him and said, "Tough. You're a tough guy, Mack Bolan. Can I tag along and load your guns for you?"

He sighed. "Hell no."

"Well ... I knew better than to ask. Mack...."

"Yeah?"

"You'll have to kill Wo Fan."

"Yeah?"

"Yeah. He's a nationalist, and my sympathies, of course, go with that cause. But he's running with the wolves now. And he's turned into a wolf himself. I suspect—no, I feel it in my bones. Wo Fan and Laurentis are up to something sneaky. I believe they are trying for a coup in the San Francisco under-world. An unholy alliance. Laurentis will help to keep the commies out. Wo Fan will help to put down the ruling Mafia family, and Laurentis will move in. I think that's it. I think that's what it's all about."

Bolan was thinking it over.

"Like Wo Fan suggested, it's a big conflict," she added quietly.

Bolan said, "And a complicated one. My war is a bit narrower than that."

"Well you'd better broaden it."

"You believe Wo Fan is a real threat? To me?"

She nodded. "Like I said, he's a wolf now. He'd stop

at nothing. If Laurentis learns that Wo Fan has been in touch with you ... and if Wo Fan decides that it would help his cause to turn you over to Laurentis ... well, I'm just saying, lookout lover. That's a hard old world out there."

Bolan consulted his wristwatch. It was a few minutes past noon. He sighed and told her, "End of détente."

"End of what?"

"Do you know the place where those girls shoot their pictures?"

"Yes."

"One more thing. Where does Barney Gibson fit into all this?"

"I'm not sure," she replied slowly, thinking about it. "He's had his problems with the mob. For years. I think he's trying to pull them down."

"On his own?"

She nodded. "Way I read it. I think he doesn't trust various people in his own department."

"Could you set up a meet between Gibson and me?"

Her eyes flared. "Whatever for?"

"A secret meet, a secure one. Could you do it?"

She stared at him with wondering eyes for a long moment, then she daintily nodded her head and told him, "I guess I could."

He said, "So do it."

Quietly, she asked, "Does that mean you trust me now?"

"That's what it means," he growled.

She squeezed his hand. "Great. That's really great."

So it was great.

The R&R was ended.

It was time, once again, to come out shooting.

140

14: THE SELL

It was an incredibly beautiful and peaceful spot, and Bolan had to wonder how often the native San Franciscans actually visited the place.

It was called the Japanese Tea Garden, and it occupied a relatively small area of Golden Gate Park. Winding footpaths through exotic shrubbery, pygmy trees and authentic Japanese statuary led the visitor beside reflecting pools and across an arched bridge where you could take your choice of an open-air tea house, a temple, or a shrine—and, yeah, this was a place where a guy could go to meet his soul.

At the moment, though, Bolan's primary interest lay in a meeting with a grizzled old maverick cop who just maybe wouldn't mind a bit of official larceny, if a greater cause were thereby being served.

Bolan was betting that Barney Gibson was that kind of cop. He was, in fact, betting his life on the idea.

He watched from behind the cover of purple sunshades and a poised teacup as the girl and the cop made their prearranged meet beside the pool. Gibson had not yet been told the reason for the meeting and—watching them now—Bolan knew the precise moment when that reason was revealed.

141

The big guy stiffened, but just across the shoulders. He did not break stride nor was there any other gross reaction, but Bolan knew.

They were talking about it now. Mary Ching, selling the Executioner. Not, he hoped, selling him out ... just selling him.

And the cop was buying. That face became immediately evident. The pair strolled on, into the enfolding garden, and just as they disappeared from view Mary hung a white flower in her hair.

Bolan promptly left his table at the tea house and went around the other way, on an intersecting path.

He got there first, per plan, and watched them approach.

Gibson was one of those guys who could fool a casual observer. On the surface he simply looked overweight, grumpy, a bit dull—maybe even a bit dumb. The head was too large, the jaw too overslung, the eyes bloodshot and masked with indifference.

But that was just the surface man.

Bolan had learned to read men, just as he read jungle signs and trails. Men, after all, were a jungle product.

All the deeper signs of Barney Gibson revealed him as definitely a cop of the old school. He wasn't a constitutional lawyer, he wasn't a civic moralist, he wasn't even a law officer. He was a cop. He wasn't there to protect anybody's civil rights, he was there to protect his town; to keep it straight; to keep it safe. He would bend the law—even break it—to do his job as he saw it.

Yeah, Bolan had known a couple of cops like Barney Gibson. Flaming, stubborn anachronisms who absolutely refused to get in step with the times. And there was still room in the world for a few Barney Gibsons.

There was no introduction, nor did the two men shake hands. Both pairs of hands, in fact, were pointedly kept in full view. The Captain said, by way of greeting, "So you're the guy. What d'you want with my town, Mister?"

Bolan solemnly told him, "Your town has a rotten smell, Captain. I sniff Mafia every step I take."

"So what's new?" the cop growled.

"Me, I'm new," the Executioner replied.

The Captain snorted. "You're practically dead, fella."

"A dead man can do things," Bolan said. "Things a living man wouldn't even think about."

"I guess you're right there. What've you got in mind?"

"I left a couple of samples around," Bolan said.

The big guy grunted. He stared at the Executioner for a moment, then admitted, "Yeah, I saw your samples. Pretty impressive. Those were just samples, eh?"

Bolan said, "Well, call it a pattern."

"I like your patterns, Mister. But somewhere else. Not here. Gives the town a bad feel. Look. I wouldn't have come if I'd known what was up. I can stretch, but not that much. You turn around and walk away from here. And keep going until you're clear out of town. That's as far as I can stretch."

"The thing is going to split wide open, Captain. Whether I leave it or not."

"What's that supposed to mean?"

"Things have become too good here. For the mob. It's time for the thieves to start falling out. They've already started."

"You have some definite knowledge of that?"

"I have," Bolan assured him. His gaze flicked to Mary Ching. "Mary can fill you in later, I don't have the time. But you better believe this. A full scale mob war is brewing here. It involves not only the organization boys but their fellow travelers as well. That means blood in the streets, and maybe a lot of innocent blood with it."

"Go on."

"So my way is much cleaner."

The shrewd old eyes were sizing him up, wondering, measuring, taking a vote. The ballot fell in the box, and Captain Gibson told the Executioner, "Okay, I'm still listening."

"I'm thinking of a clean sweep, from the bottom to the top. I'll take the top and leave the bottom for you."

"That's damn nice of you."

"Be realistic," Bolan argued. "You'll never wrap up the big boys and you know it. And as long as they're up there, this town will be crawling with torpedoes and leeches of every variety. When the big boys fall, the influence falls with them. You'll need to set up annexes to your jails to handle the load."

"So why tell me about it?" The guy was interested, though, definitely interested. "Why don't you just go ahead and do it. Why consult me first?"

"I might need your help."

"Uh huh, I guess I saw that coming."

"Nothing open, nothing that would put you on a spot. I just want you to pass a few words around for me."

"And what are those?"

Bolan smiled, for the first time during the meeting.

"Would you say that we've come to an agreement in principle?"

The cop smiled back, and it was a hideous thing. He wasn't used to smiling, and it moved all the wrinkles the wrong way. "You might say that."

"Okay," Bolan said. "I'll be in touch with you through Mary."

"Why not get it all on the table right now? I'm here, you're here, let's have it."

"Not yet," Bolan told him. "I'll be in touch."

"Hell, you've got me dangling, fella. What the hell have you got in mind?"

"You'll know very soon," Bolan assured him.

He grabbed Mary's arm and they left there in a hurry.

Yeah, very soon. The whole thing would be cracking . . . very soon now.

"Say that again," requested Leo Turrin's troubled voice, all the way from Pittsfield.

"Something wrong, Leo? You don't sound too good," Bolan decided.

"No, I'll tell you later. I'm just not sure I heard you right. What was that again?"

"I said I want you to get a message to Augie Marinello."

"In your name?" the *Caporegime* asked.

Bolan said, "No, just in my spirit. Don't make the impression that it came from me."

"What do you have in common with the Lord of the East?" Turrin wanted to know. He still sounded troubled . . . almost cold.

"Blood, maybe," Bolan said, chuckling. "He's still the big boss?"

145

"More or less," Turrin replied in that curiously masked tone. "What he says at council usually turns out to be the way things go. What kind of a message, Sarge?"

"I want him to know there's a conspiracy brewing on the west coast. Top drawer stuff. Big enough to wreck the whole arm. The shot heard 'round the world, that sort of thing. Following?"

"Yeah. What's the pitch?"

"A new coalition," Bolan replied.

"Coalition of what?"

"Try the ChiComs with Daddy DeMarco as a starter. How does that grab?"

"Easy, easy," Turrin said. "I've told you things have been in the wind."

"But you didn't tell me what sort of things, Leo."

"Right, well ... hell. Okay. Here's the way I'm reading. The boys hate the hell out of the commies. You know?"

Bolan said, "I know. But business before pleasure. Right?"

"So right. Business before anything. I hear they've been trading. Mostly in narcotics, but other things too. Uh, Mack ... what coalition?"

"It's only in my mind, right now. But it could be for real, Leo. It could be. I'd like for Marinello to think it is for damn sure."

"Why?"

"Because I want him to shake the hell out of Daddy DeMarco."

"Okay. What's the plot?"

"The plot is simply this. DeMarco is Mr. King's boy ... even more, maybe, than he's the organization's boy. And Mr. King has big ideas for the West Coast.

146

With trade routes to the Chinese mainland now almost a certain event in the near future, Mr. King is moving swiftly to dominate the entire import picture, and the exports to China as well. Not just narcotics, not just contraband, but the big sweep, everything. The picture forming?"

The man in Pittsfield was evincing definite interest now. "Yeah. Keep going. Uh, you're saying this Mr. King is coming out in competition with the regular mob setup."

"Right, in direct competition. Would this suggest a conflict of interest to your mind? Concerning DeMarco and his close ties with King?"

"Sure. Is this for real?"

"It could be. There's a certain old Chinese gentleman here who is definitely worried about something pretty close to that. So worried, in fact, that he has already formed a counter-coalition."

"Who with?"

"There's a dime-store hood here called Franco Laurentis. Know him?"

"That guy. Yeah. Crazy Franco. They call him that because he's always had a Napoleon complex. Thinks he was born to rule the world or something, or so the story goes."

"Perfect," Bolan said.

"Yeah, well, he's also DeMarco's enforcer."

"Even better yet. He's pulling something cute on the old man, Leo. It sounds like he's trying for a takeover—or something very close to that. Uh, get this name now, Daniel Wo Fan." Bolan spelled it. "Local Chinese honcho, very strong ties with Taiwan. He and Franco have been cozying it. They're interlaced in various projects around the bay area. I believe Franco has made an agreement with Wo Fan ... to kill the ChiCom trade."

Turrin whistled across the connection. There was a momentary silence, then he said, "The guy must *really* be crazy if he's trying to cross DeMarco. The *Don* is old, but he's a hell of a long ways from dead. He's eaten guys like Franco Laurentis for casual snacks."

"That's the whole idea, Leo."

"Yeah, yeah, I get the drift. Well ... hell, it's a great idea, Sarge. I would guess that Franco is the head torpedo in charge of stopping *you*. If, uh, if he's thinking of crossing the old man, this would be his golden opportunity."

"Exactly what I'm thinking. You know what to say to Marinello now, Leo?"

Sourly, Turrin replied, "I do. I just wish I could be out there to see the results."

Bolan said, "Well ... if I get luck, Leo, I'll give you a blow-by-blow account."

"Do that. Listen, wait, don't hang up yet."

It was coming now, the trouble in Leo Turrin's voice. Bolan asked him, "You ready to tell me about your problem now?"

"Yeah. I've, uh, got something disturbing to tell you, but. ..."

"But what?"

"I don't want you to get all upset. I mean, maybe it's nothing at all."

A chill chased itself down Bolan's spine. He said, "Let's have it."

"Well, Johnny and Val have taken off somewhere."

Something ticked loose in Bolan's brain. He said, "Since when?"

"Since I tried to get in touch this morning. I wanted

them to know I'd talked to you. They . . . just aren't there, Sarge. No one at the school remembers seeing either of them since early last night."

Bolan's guts were coming unglued. "Their clothes, Leo, what about—"

"Hard to tell. They left some behind, yeah, but there's no way of knowing if they took any away with them. I mean. . . ."

Bolan's ears were roaring. Woodenly, he said, "You mean they could have been snatched."

"It's possible. But there are a lot of other possibilities, too. You remember I told you Val was agitating for a meet. They could have bugged out of there early this morning. The Frisco news was all over the television—you know how the home town follows you. I mean, I think maybe they're headed that way, Sarge. I think Val just decided, hell, to set up her own meet."

Bolan muttered, "I don't believe Val would do that. Not with Johnny along, anyway. She knows what a risk it is. No. I can't buy that, Leo."

The panic was edging clearly into Turrin's voice now. "God, I've been living with my ear to the ground all day, Sarge. I haven't heard a rumble from the boys. Not one. If somebody got to them, then they're being mighty damn quiet about it."

Bolan's voice was very cold and lifeless as he said, "Leo, please keep that ear busy. If you hear anything, the tiniest whisper, get word to me immediately."

"Okay, you know I will. What's the best path?"

"Call that television correspondent in New York. We have an arrangement. Just tell him it's a windmill emergency. He'll understand, and he'll get the message on the network newscast. You know the guy?"

"Yeah, I remember."

"Okay."

"Sarge . . . Mack . . . Goddammit. I'm sorry."

"Not your fault, Leo. I guess I've always known this might happen someday. I—"

"We don't know for sure it's happened yet."

"Right, you're right. Uh, thanks for—thanks, Leo. Keep alert, eh?"

"I will. And I'll get this other thing into Augie Marinello right away."

"I'll appreciate it."

"Yeah."

Bolan hung up. He stared thoughtfully at his hands for a moment, then he left the phone booth and rejoined Mary Ching on the sidewalk.

Her eyes searched his face, then she slipped a hand into his and said, "It didn't go well."

"It went swell," he told her.

"But you're wearing the death mask."

"I am?"

"You are. Was it a hard sell?"

"It was an easy sell," he replied quietly.

"What, then?"

"A personal matter. Forget it, let me do the worrying."

"Nothing's changed?"

"Nothing," he assured her, "is changed. The hit is on."

"What's next?" she wondered aloud, still giving him the searching gaze.

"The porno girls."

"What?—oh! The kids."

"Yeah. I just want to reassure myself about them. It can be a hell of a tough world for kids."

She whispered, "Yes, it can."

Something, Mary Ching knew, was very much out of place inside Mack Bolan. It was like, suddenly, he was a total stranger. Cold, hard ... deadly.

She pressed against him as they went up the street, and she told him, "Hey, tough guy, I wish I knew what that contact said to you on the phone."

Bolan did not reply.

She tried again. "I mean, okay, you sold him your package. But what did he sell you in exchange?"

"He sold me," Bolan quietly told her, "the idea that this is one hell of a lousy war. Especially for women and children."

Whatever that meant. Mary felt a prickling at her scalp. It wasn't what Mr. Tough said ... it was the voice he said it with.

In a small voice, she asked him, "After you've reassured yourself about the kids ... what's next after that?"

"Brushfire," he said.

"What?"

He showed her a smile which was more like death stretching itself. "A Brushfire is next after that, Mary."

She knew it was an understatement. What was next, she was convinced, was a roaring conflagration.

15: THE SAVE

It was three o'clock and only ten hours into the California battle when the warwagon crept to the curb outside the production studio on upper Geary Street. Bolan was wearing slacks and a shirt open at the neck, crepe soled shoes, a conservative blazer, and the Beretta Belle snugged within easy access.

He parked in a loading zone directly in front of the studio and gave Mary Ching a curt nod of the head. "Try it," he said.

She exited and went to the studio entrance, then returned quickly to the vehicle. Her eyes were large and worried as she reported, "Closed, locked. Shouldn't be. They're usually working right into the early evening."

He asked, "Could they have finished, wrapped it up?"

Worriedly, she replied, "Hardly. Just started yesterday."

He said, "Okay. Here's what you do. Sit right here. Don't budge for anything and don't let anybody move you away. If you hear gunfire, though, beat it quick. Go exactly one block north on Van Ness and wait for me there, even if you have to double park. Time it, and if I'm not there within two minutes, then you split. Every hour on the hour after that, cruise past the corner of Powell and Geary. You have that?"

"I have it," she assured him.

Bolan left her then and proceeded directly to the studio entrance.

The door was mostly glass, not designed for extraordinary security precautions, with an ordinary mechanical lock, the type that is built into the inner hardware. It silently came apart under the first probe of his handy little tool, and he let himself in.

There was a reception area with a low wrought-iron railing to one side, a freight counter on the other. Behind the railing was a desk and a couple of cheap couches; swung off farther into the reception area were two private offices, an unfamiliar Italian name lettered upon each one.

There were no signs of life in that forward area.

Set into the far wall was a rugged looking door of solid construction, no visible hardware. Stenciled across it in thick white letters was the admonition:

STUDIO
ABSOLUTELY NO ENTRY

Bolan found the secret to the door at the reception desk, via a push-button which was hung to the underside. He pressed it. The door hummed a brief note and cracked open.

He went through without pause and into the darkened interior of the studio. It was a bit larger than he'd expected, long but rather narrow in the approaches with—probably—dressing rooms and offices to either side. At the far rear everything opened up again and it was a single large warehouse-like sound stage with overhead lofts and scattered with photographic and sound equipment.

Bolan noted three small "sets"—one had a thin layer of sand spread along the cardboard backdrop of what might pass as an ocean if something of more optical interest were placed in front of it—like, say, a beautiful nude young body. The other two sets were mockups of, respectively, a bedroom and a living room. Both were rather grim scenes; Bolan would not have liked to live there.

The only lights in present operation were a pair of white spots on the bedroom set.

A cluster of guys were standing across the front of the set and blocking most of the view into the bedroom. It wasn't so blocked, though, that Bolan couldn't catch a glimpse of a couple of scared looking kids seated cross-legged on the bed. They wore white terrycloth robes which probably would have bottomed out around their thighs if they'd been standing, and that's all they were wearing.

The guys were mostly in shadow, but Bolan could see that they were not dressed for either bedroom or studio work. There were six of them, and the suits they were wearing were not silk, but they may as well have been. These were Chinese boys, and they looked as ornery as anything Franco Laurentis could have fielded.

A seventh guy was up on the set, standing beside the bed, posturing angrily and addressing the girls in quietly furious tones. He was an Occidental, and he wore a silk suit too.

The coalition, yeah.

Bolan moved quietly onto the beach set, found the

154

lights, swiveled them about to his best advantage, and ignited them.

Everybody in and around the bedroom set came rapidly alive. The six Chinese boys were less demonstrative than any, but even they came around in a fanlike confrontation, plainly warlike, arms suddenly stiff and ready for anything.

The guy at the bed whirled about and did a quick little two-step off the platform like a bedroom phantom caught in the act. The girls grabbed each other, hid their heads and simply clung together.

All others were looking directly into Bolan's lights, so he could have appeared to them as no more than a vague shadow somewhere in the background.

The voice was not vague, however; it was harsh, and laden with ice as it commanded, "Cool it!"

"Who's there?" silksuit snarled.

"Death, if that's what you want, Clyde," Bolan promised.

Two of the China boys twitched. Bolan drilled them cleanly, with two sighing little *phu-uts* that were grouped so close as to sound like one, and then there were four.

The survivors stood rigid, frozen, not even interested in the condition of their fallen brethren, and the white torpedo took a tentative step forward, both hands stretched forward in a placating gesture.

"Hey wait, wait!" he urged, in a voice quivering with sudden respect.

"You wait," Bolan countered. "Send those girls out here, and don't be cute about it."

"You uh, that's all you want, eh?"

"Right now, yeah," Bolan assured him.

"Shit, guy, they're not worth it."

155

"They are to me," insisted the death voice. "Send them."

The guy sent them. Panda and Cynthey scampered panting and sobbing into the waiting darkness behind the spots. In the momentary close-up, Bolan had received an instant understanding of what they'd been put through. Those cute faces were now welted and puffy, bloated from a combination of blows and tears, and terribly, terribly unhappy. A dried trickle of blood remained at the corner of Cynthie's mouth.

As they hurried past, he quietly instructed them, "The van, right outside. Mary's waiting."

He gave them until the door up there opened and closed, then he told the coalition of five, "Now you guys draw straws to see who'll be the first man out behind me. Or else lean together for awhile and live to remember."

He withdrew in a quiet backpedal, and apparently the coalition had decided to lean together. There was no pursuit. The warwagon was fired up and Mary Ching was riding the clutch in a slow crawl when he casually opened the door and slid in beside her.

"Go," he said.

The two kids were huddled together on the rear deck, alternately crying and laughing in mutual hysteria, and Mary had taken the corner and proceeded several blocks up Van Ness before Bolan could edge an intelligent word into it.

"Tell me a safe place to drop you," he demanded.

"Sausalito," Cynthey replied without hesitation.

"You sure?"

She bobbed her head in an emphatic reply. "Our friends will take care of us. I just dare those goons to. . . ."

156

"Sure you wouldn't rather have police protection?"

Both girls shuddered at that suggestion, and Bolan dropped it.

He turned a sigh to Mary Ching. "You know the place?"

"I know," she said, and she made it sound almost like Bolan saying it.

He scowled, freshened the Belle, and the porno girls plus two headed for the Golden Gate.

The story did not need to be told, but they wanted to tell it, so Bolan let them. It was nothing new, the usual routine, an incautious word dropped in a dangerous place, a visiting delegation of hard-eyed and equally quick-fisted inquisitors. They'd closed the place down and sent everybody home ... everybody but the two female "stars"—and two hours of mind-blowing hell had ensued.

They'd wanted to know everything the girls knew—which they got very quickly—and a lot of things the girls could never know. When the proper answers were not forthcoming, there were hideous threats and stories of mutilated young bodies floating out through the Golden Gate, and there were blows and various other physical indignities.

None of the delegation were ready to accept the truth that the girls actually knew nothing whatever concerning Mack Bolan's plans and/or present whereabouts. Apparently they had come prepared to spend the night—and no doubt would have—had not Bolan himself provided the answer regarding his present whereabouts.

Cynthey was effusively grateful for the rescue; Panda was surly and resentful of the fact that Bolan's shadow had entered and clouded their lives. As the story went on, it became apparent that Panda had been the one with the leaky mouth. She was clearly jealous of the impression Bolan had made on the other girl, and it was during an angry denunciation of "all men including your fancy Mack Bolan" at lunch time, when the wrong ears were listening and their hell began.

Bolan did not feel responsible, except in the sense that any human is responsible for another. He had neither sought their company nor given any moves to maintain it. He had warned them of the value of silence, and they had blown it. As a result, they had endangered not only themselves, but Mary Ching as well, and they could quite easily have become the instruments of Bolan's downfall.

On the other hand, he certainly felt no resentment toward the porno girls. They were, after all, just kids. He was just damned glad that he'd gotten to them in time, and that the thing had worked out as well as it did.

He did feel strongly responsible, however, for a pair of somewhat different people back East. They were tied to him by the invisible threads of mutual love and hazard, and their beloved lives had been plunged into a torment of furtive existence—hiding that they may live—and all because of Bolan's lousy war.

And the guy had the nerve to ask him if it was *important!*

Then there was that other responsibility sitting there coolly beside him, a China doll who had also become special and was dangerously compromised by Bolan's war. And he was dragging her deeper into it with each passing moment.

So it was a lot of baloney; a guy could not stand alone, not absolutely alone, not so long as he lived in a world of people. The people were what the war was all about. And some of them, here and there along the way, were going to get burned. There was no way around that idea; there was no way to stand absolutely alone.

Important? Yeah, Corporal Phillips, it was damned important.

He told Mary Ching, "Your humble pad is now death row. Avoid it, write it off, don't ever go back there again."

Mary's eyes found those pathetic kids in the rearview mirror; they found the tortured misery in the Executioner's gaze; she nodded her head and told him, "Okay. Okay."

She knew, now, what Mack Bolan was made of.

Sausalito is a picturesque little village lying directly across from San Francisco on the Gate's north shore. Bolan had spent a weekend there once, shortly after Korea. Under another time and mood, he would have greeted the quaint beauty of "the Portofino of the West" with a nostalgic appreciation; on this trip he felt merely tense and anxious to have the bedsy twins off his hands and mind. His numbers were getting crowded and—although San Francisco was only minutes behind him—he was a bit irritable over the fact that he'd left the town behind just when all the numbers were beginning to come together.

The warwagon, under the sure guidance of Mary Ching, was picking its way clear of the bridge approach and winding onto a narrow shoreside road, circling onto the bay.

He should have received the initial ding when the first huge signboard blurred across his vision, proclaiming in red letters a foot high, SAVE THE BAY— but with everything else that had transpired that day, he wasn't as quick to draw the connection. Several signs and as many jogs in the road later, they came upon the houseboat, about a hundred yards off the road, snuggled into a cozy inlet and tied by heavy hawsers to a couple of accommodating trees.

It was small, as some houseboats go, but the letters blazed across it from stem to stern—BAYSAVERS— would be a difficult item for anyone to miss—and this time there was no miss inside Bolan's brain.

Already, though, Mary was swinging the van onto the little trail to the boat and Cynthey was on her knees directly behind him and proudly declaring, "That's it, that's the home where the heart is."

It was also a home where a lot of hell was likely to be unleashed, and it didn't even take an executioner's mentality to recognize that harsh fact of winner-take-all warfare.

He snarled at Cynthey, "Is this also the home of Baysavers Incorporated?"

Her eyes were baffled and recoiling from the savagery of his tone as she stammered, "S-sure, well n-no, I mean, Mr. Vericci gave us the boat. You've heard of him?" She shrank back all the way, reading the truth of Bolan's eyes, and wailed, "Oh, no!"

Oh yeah. He'd heard of him.

Bolan would never cease to marvel at the fantastic interconnections in the world of Mafia, and the way they always seemed to reach out and tie up a guy when he was least expecting it.

Touch one and you reach them all, that was the

lesson the Executioner had learned many hot battles ago, but one which he apparently had not learned quite well enough.

A heavy car had already pulled crosswise onto the trail behind them, blocking the way out.

Movements, now—excitedly surreptitious ones— were taking place down there around that boat ... and, yeah, all the numbers had crowded together on that narrow trail outside of Sausalito.

His leg pushed Mary's aside and his foot found the brake pedal to stand the warwagon on her nose.

He knew now, yeah, why he'd been feeling so irritable.

He had goofed, he had overlooked something, and that little sentinel of the inner mind had been screaming into his blindness that he had left something behind in San Francisco.

It wasn't his heart, either.

He'd left his caution and his combat quick and maybe his whole damn lousy war.

He'd become weary of the stand alone.

He'd ridden blithely and blindly into the most outrageously obvious set-up of them all—and he'd come in stupid, deaf, and feeling sorry for himself.

In a voice quivering with self-disgust, he commanded, "Out Mary's side and into the dirt, all of you! Hit the water on my signal and stay the hell clear!"

And then Bolan tried for the only save he knew.

He came out shooting.

16: STYLE

Bolan exploded through the rear door of the war-wagon, a combat belt slung hastily across his neck and a blazing burpgun in his hands.

The immediate target was that rear guard vehicle with its six occupants, and it was obvious that they had not expected anything like this. The range was less than fifty yards, far less than the maximum effective for the combat machine gun. The assault caught them on the seat of their pants and clawing like hell to get out of that sitting target; their first few rounds were hasty and purely reactive.

Bolan himself was firing for cover, not for effect. He moved out behind the blazing attack and found the so-so shelter of a stubby tree before the boys could pull their wits back together.

By the time they had their doors open, he had snatched an ornament from the combat belt and base-balled an HE grenade along the course to facilitate their scrambling exit. It hit the ground a few yards shy and rolled on home, exploding directly beneath the vehicle and lifting it to full spring travel in a rocking-rolling motion.

Two guys were still inside at that instant, and the others were no more than a pace away. Two of the outsiders were flattened, hard, by the blast. The other two were reeling away from there and firing handguns at the moon. The burpgun cut them down before they could get their legs fully beneath them.

One of the guys still in the vehicle was screaming bloody murder ... and then the secondary explosion came, the gas tank letting go with a horrible whooosh and sending a horizontal jet of fire streaking along the undercarriage like a flame-thrower. The car came up off its wheels, riding that cushion of fire, and the screamer lost it all in a final high-pitched gurgle.

That took care of the rear.

If you wanta play, guys, it's best to bring your own ball.

Bolan was already running along the treeline in a reverse course toward the houseboat.

As he passed the van he shouted, "Okay, hit the drink!"—and again he turned the burper loose, desiring only to attract all eyes to that flaming muzzle and away from the girls.

It was a successful diversion. He was drawing plenty of fire.

Something tore through the fabric of his coat and another sizzling chunk practically parted his hair.

Bolan dived in behind a rock, about midway between the warwagon and the boat, and he reloaded the heated burper while he ran a spot on the enemy.

Some clown was on the roof of the houseboat with a lever-action rifle. That boat had a flat, square roof, absolutely flat, with nothing more than a couple of 3-inch stovepipes and a TV antenna to serve as cover.

Another guy was kneeling just off the gangway, taking cover behind a trash barrel, and plinking at Bolan with a small caliber pistol.

163

The woods in front of the boat, now, were another matter altogether. Most of their firepower seemed to have been concentrated out there. Muzzle flashes were visible from about five widely scattered points, grouped in multiples, and they were laying a withering fire on him, keeping him pinned behind the rock.

Bolan risked a craning inspection of the bay, and he was partially satisfied to note two girlish heads bobbing around out there just offshore.

It was the two kids.

Mary Ching was nowhere in evidence.

Cynthey seemed to be stroking for the houseboat. As Bolan watched, she paused to tread water and cup her hands for a shout toward her goal. "Everybody out!" she screamed in a high falsetto. "Alla you kids get out of there!"

Somebody was thinking.

The guy on the roof levered a shot at Cynthey.

Bolan splattered him with a single burst from the burper, then he yelled, "Cynthey, stay under!"

It was an unnecessary direction. A glistening bare bottom rose to the surface as she went for depth, and she was gone in a flash. Panda, too, knew where safety was, and she immediately followed suit.

San Francisco Bay had cold, cold water—and Bolan felt a bit bad about that—but it was still the best place for them, especially since both seemed in pretty good control of their environment. There was no control over that other environment—not for the noncombatant—and Bolan had not wanted them in that fire zone.

He cast about for a glimpse of Mary Ching and came up with zero.

Behind him the plug vehicle was now in roaring

flames and sending a dense cloud of black smoke soaring skyward.

It was a bad situation. He could have gone on out through that dissolved rear plug, sure, and left everybody to pick up their own marbles. But Bolan just did not play the game that way.

So here he was—pinned down. Probably 15 or 20 guns out there somewhere. Several more on the boat.

A Mexican stand-off could work no way but against Bolan. The heart of the village was less than a half-mile away; there would be an official reaction to that smoke and rattling firefight, and it could come damn quick.

On the other hand, no one man could successfully rush those woods, nor could he remain content for long with merely good cover, cops or not. Someone was probably already circling around to get behind him.

So . . . .

Bolan put the burpgun aside and hauled out the big silver blaster. A sniping mission ... with a handgun? Why not? The Auto Mag was certainly no ordinary handgun.

He showed himself and waited for a muzzle flash, and it wasn't much of a wait. Several came immediately. He tracked onto the most likely target and sent 240 grains right back at him, targeting right on the flash.

The guy behind that muzzle came immediately into full view, pitching sideways and down and out of the picture.

Bolan bobbed up again, and another exchange of fire produced a like result.

It was a hell of a grim way to play Russian roulette. Somebody else out there was getting the same idea, and they were losing. There was movement out there—a shifting about.

Then a rattling burst sounded to Bolan's rear. He was swinging about to give the shortarm sniper a sniff of the situation when a guy fell away from the side of a rock, up on his flank, and the China doll stepped out from behind the van to sweep that entire side with a blazing machine-pistol.

It was too late to do anything but try to cover her.

Bolan rose to full height and extended the Auto Mag in a firing-range stance. The big piece boomed and belched fire in a rapid unload—and when the clip was empty Mary was up in the rocks on his exposed flank, in good cover now and firing selectively at specific targets.

She was good, she was damned good, and Bolan knew that the tide of battle had turned.

There was considerable movement out there now, quick movements in the direction of the boat.

Many heads were now visible in the water, Bolan reckoned about a dozen in the quick scan, and it seemed that Cynthey's buddies had joined her for the swim.

He called up to Mary, "Okay! Hold it!"

She called back, "Okay!"

The woodchucks were bailing out, and Bolan counted them as they scampered out of the woods and scurried across the gangway onto the houseboat. Eight left. Great. He let them go, giving them the boat, his mind already drawing upon a certain way to cut short the stalemate.

"Stay alert!" he warned Mary Ching.

She waved at him.

He thrust the Auto Mag into his belt and scooped

166

up the burper, then moved into the trees and worked his way downrange toward the boat.

It wasn't really a boat, at all. It was just a big square raft with walls and a roof, a small porch which overhung the water in the gangway area, and a narrow walkway around the sides.

The idea was firmly crystallized now and, from a range of about ten yards, Bolan opened fire on the nearest mooring tree.

The big hawser popped dust and fuzz, then threads and strands; finally the cable parted with a groan.

One end of the houseboat immediately swung away from the shore and stretched itself toward the open bay, dragging the gangway with it.

Mary Ching, the China gunner, let out a whoop of delighted encouragement.

Concerned faces appeared at the windows of the boat, and someone in there yelled, "What the hell is this?"

Bolan was already circling toward the other mooring tree. He let it have another clip from the burpgun. This time the rope cable parted with a twang and an explosive pop, and BAYSAVERS quickly drifted away in an idle exploration of that which it would save.

A youthful voice from the water yelled, "Our boat, our boat!"

Another shouted, "Let it go! *Bon voyage*, freaks!"

Bolan didn't feel too badly about the kids' boat. The Coast Guard would drag it back to them . . . if something more disastrous didn't occur before they made the scene.

And there were more immediate problems.

A distant siren was wailing down on them, descending from the direction of Sausalito.

The crew of BAYSAVERS, now at a relatively safe distance from the fire zone, were manning the rail and staring back at the receding shoreline.

Bolan met his lady gunner at the van, and they quickly stowed their weapons with a stony silence.

Bolan moved to the driver's side while Mary crawled in through the rear gate and secured that end, then she slid in beside him as he cranked the engine.

The van had taken numerous punctures but, miraculously, all the glass was intact.

She said, "Well. It still runs."

Bolan replied, "You see, we have this understanding."

He was see-sawing about in the turnaround when a glistening and shivering pair of porno girls descended on them.

Bolan poked his head out the window and strove to keep his gaze at eye level as he told them, "Sorry to hit and run, but it's time to buzz. The fuzz, you know."

Cynthey showed him a pained smile. "Just wanted you to know," she panted. "I recognized some of those hoods. Two of them . . . I've seen several times with Thomas Vericci. He's a director of—"

Bolan said, "I know, Baysavers Ink. He's also a Mafia honcho, Cynthey. Don't let people con you like that."

She jerked her head and told him, "I'm just getting that idea. I think I've been conned about a lot of things." She screwed her battered face around and said, "Listen. I didn't know about this. I think they just collaborated on this thing. You know? While they

168

pushed us around on Geary, these others came out here to cover all possibilities."

Bolan smiled soberly. "That's the way I figure it." The siren was getting louder and Mary Ching was beginning to fidget. He said, "You kids better buzz out of here. There could be a return visit."

"What do we tell the fuzz?"

He handed her a marksman's medal. "Give them this. It's all the explanation you'll need."

Panda the Bare blurted, "Bolan! Mr. Bolan! Thanks!"

He grinned. "Stay cool and lay low. For awhile, anyway."

He dug the wheels in and burned away from there. They made it to the bridge approach seconds ahead of the official vehicles, and he turned a tight smile to the fastest gun in Chinatown.

"I guess we made it," he told her.

"Is that all you have to say to me, Mr. Taciturn?"

The smile loosened somewhat as he replied, "We're alive, aren't we? What can I add to that?"

She leaned against him and hugged his arm.

"You're right," she murmured. "What is there to add."

He relented. "Okay. You were great. You're welcome to cover my flank any time."

"Gee," she replied with a wry face. "You just made my whole day."

"Not quite." They were rolling with the traffic now, crossing the big span. "It's time for that call to Barney Gibson. You remember what to say?"

She twisted the rose-petal face into a disgusted scowl. "Of course I remember what to say."

169

"Okay. I'll drop you at the marina. Make the call and then get clear."

She growled, delicately, way up at the top of her throat, and told him, "And I get screwed without even a kiss."

He grinned at her and said, "What?"

"*Damned* if I will. That phone call, old heart of rocks, is going to cost you one hellish kiss."

Bolan chuckled, and a minute later he pulled out of the traffic from the bridge and nosed into a little observation area.

She got her hellish kiss, then a couple more, then he gruffly shoved her toward the door and told her, "Make the call."

Her eyes were all deep pools of understanding and tender concern.

"You feeling better about everything now?" she huskily asked him.

He nodded and replied, "Some."

A procession of police cars screamed past, headed for the bridge and reflecting the setting sun off their windshields.

Bolan thought he spotted a black face in the lead car.

Mary watched the procession pass, then she slipped outside, leaned back in for a final look, and told him, "That was quick. I'll bet they're barricading the Golden Gate. Doesn't that make you feel important?"

He told her, "Not exactly. Uh, if I get lucky, lady gunner, let's meet you know where."

She said, "A thundering herd of dinosaurs couldn't keep me away. Mack ... dammit ... don't be so wild. Take care of yourself."

He gave her a solemn wink.

She closed the door and stepped back. He beeped the horn at her and swung back into traffic.

Most of it was headed the other way. It was that time of day, and the city was emptying itself.

But not entirely.

The plot was simple, sure, but Bolan was hoping it would keep a very select number of people inside the big, gutsy city this evening.

Yeah, a very select number.

Barney Gibson would not let him down, Bolan felt sure of that.

But it still was not all in place and . . . no Mary, Mack Bolan was not feeling that much better yet. Not yet. It was time for the Executioner to add his ante to the growing pot.

It was time to pay a call on an ambitious hood who thought he was destined to rule the earth.

Then maybe, the Executioner would feel a lot better about his world.

It was time to show some style to the king of style.

He stepped out of the private elevator and iced the foyer sentry with the muzzle end of the Belle, firmly against the forehead.

"It's up to you if you live awhile," Bolan coldly announced.

The guy was a hard item, sure, and those eyes didn't flinch much but he was thinking about long life and happier times. The voice was strained with controlled fury as he replied, "Sure, tough, let's live a little."

Bolan asked, "Who's in there?"

"Just th' boss."

"No one else?"

"Would I lie to you, guy? At a time like this?"

Bolan promised him, "If you're wrong, silk, I'll finish you on my way out."

The bodyguard felt that perhaps he should explain, to cinch the deal. In a cordial tone, he reported, "They're all out chasing your tracks. He's in there alone, buy it. Who'd of thought you'd just waltz in here? In broad daylight yet?"

"You don't like the guy much," Bolan decided.

The hardman shrugged, but carefully. "Pay's the same whether I like 'im or not. There's no pay for dead men."

If the guy was expecting a pat on the back, he was sorely disappointed. The Executioner felled him with a jolt to the throat, then made sure with a Beretta slap to the head.

He fished the key from a special pocket and quietly let himself into the penthouse suite.

A stereo tape system in the corner was recreating the Nashville sound, with Johnny Cash artistically relating the glory of the old days of railroading. Bright lights were on behind the bar. The bar itself was littered with soiled glasses and overflowing ashtrays, and it reeked of stale beer.

Franco had been entertaining.

Bolan passed on through the living room and into the glass side of the joint. All of San Francisco and goodly portions of Alameda and Marin Counties were laid out there for inspection.

The sliding doors to the terrace were open. Bolan paused beside a planter with a real live tree embedded in it and called out, "Franco?"

The enforcer was on his terrace, leaning against the

safety wall on both forearms, enjoying the sight and smell in the late-afternoon sun of his city.

He was in shirtsleeves and a pearl-handled snub was clipped to the belt at his waist.

Franco turned his head only, about halfway around, and said, "Yeah, who's there?"

"Me," Bolan replied quietly.

"Me—who the hell?" Franco asked nastily, turning fully around.

Bolan had moved through the doorway. He was standing there with the Belle extended for easy viewing, and he must have presented an unsettling sight.

The enforcer jerked upright and took one staggering step to the side, his hand snapping up with the movement in an automatic reaction.

Bolan growled, "Uh-uh!"—freezing the hand with the suggested threat. It hung there, beside the pearl handle, clawing impotently and helplessly at the air.

"Let's talk this over," Laurentis suggested in a strangling voice.

Bolan said, "Talk is cheap, Franco."

"We can make it expensive. Uh, I like your style, man. I really do. Always have. Look. I don't blame you for hitting the old man, Christ knows I don't. I been thinking about something like that myself. I mean it."

"Save the long-winded hope, Franco," Bolan suggested. "There's nobody here but you and me. So let's talk expensive. How expensive?"

"Huh?"

"How much are you willing to gamble on talk?"

The ambitious hood stared at his visitor for a long moment, trying to read him, and Bolan could feel the cogs turning behind those eyes. Presently he replied, "I guess we could work out most anything. Couldn't we?"

"Not quite," Bolan said in that icy voice. "Here's the choice you can make. Certain death right here and now. Or a chance to get away slightly dirtied and no doubt marked for death later. If you want to gamble, I'll give you that much of an out."

The eyes had narrowed, almost closed completely. "I don't get you."

"I'm going to drill you right between the eyes and shove your carcass over that wall there."

Franco stiffened again and threw a quick glance toward the city. He must have decided that there was little style in going that way. He didn't want to join the damned thing, he wanted to own it.

"Or what?" he asked tensely.

"Or you can walk in there to your telephone. Pick it up. Make two calls. One to Tom the Broker. The other to Vince Ciprio."

The guy nervously wet his lips. "And then what do I say?"

"You offer them a chance to come over with you, *under* you. You make it convincing as hell, or it's over the wall."

"I don't ... I don't get you."

"Sure you do. Everybody in town knows what you've been setting up, Franco. You and Wo Fan."

The guy was starting to jerk around like a puppet trying to shake off his strings. He started to say something, choked, then tried it again. "You're telling me to slit my own throat, guy."

Bolan smiled the thin grim smile of death. "Depends on how you want to go, Franco. My way. Or

174

yours. With a chance. An outside chance, sure. But
. . . for a savvy boy like you, at least a chance. You've
got thirty seconds to decide."

"Well wait . . . ."

"Go for your gun if you'd like to, Franco."

"No I—wait a minute!"

With ice forming at his lips, Bolan assured him,
"Thirty seconds, twenty-five now."

"So how do I know you won't rub me anyway, after
I've called?"

"That's part of the gamble, Franco. Twenty seconds."

"You'll *have* to rub me. You won't just walk away
and leave me standing here!"

"Fifteen seconds. I'll help you this much. I plan to
lock you in a closet. I'll leave you a penknife. I figure
I'll be well clear before you can cut your way out.
Time's up, Franco."

The Belle raised higher and closed the distance by
about six inches. Bolan gave him a clear view, right
up the silencer.

"Okay! Okay! I'll play your silly fuckin' game!"

Bolan closed on him, lifted the pearled snub—
holster and all—and dropped it into his own pocket.

"The phone, Franco," he said coldly. "Go cut your
rotten throat."

That, Franco knew, was pure style.

17: LEANING TOGETHER

By eight o'clock the DeMarco mansion had become the scene of much coming and going, tense consultations, and urgent telephone messages.

Thomas Vericci and Vince Ciprio were very much on the scene, as were many of their lieutenants and hardmen.

The developments which gave rise to this feverish pace of activity occurred in a chronological sequence which was roughly as follows:

At a little before 4:00 PM, an urgent long-distance conference connection was established between San Francisco, Buffalo, Washington, Philadelphia, Boston, and three separate offices in New York City.

During this conference, Roman DeMarco was advised to cool things down in his town, particularly a rumored impending territorial war. It was also suggested that the *commissione* would view with harsh disfavor any outside arrangements of DeMarco's which could conceivably compromise the organization's intra-relationships.

Mack Bolan's name did not enter the conversation.

Roman DeMarco quit this telephone conference in a rage.

At about five o'clock both Vericci and Ciprio, at

their respective offices, received telephone calls from Crazy Franco Laurentis. Each received the identical ultimatum—join Laurentis in a move to overthrow Roman DeMarco or take the slide with the *Capo*.

Both underbosses soberly promised to give Laurentis their decision before midnight, and then each promptly telephoned *Don* DeMarco to report this curious development.

DeMarco immediately sent a "delegation" to "the top of the joint" to summon the crazy man to a consultation with the *Capo*.

The delegation reported back that Franco's suite was deserted and that there was no clue to the whereabouts of Crazy Franco.

At 5:40 PM a "paper conference" involving DeMarco, Vericci and Ciprio was conducted in the study of the DeMarco Mansion. A contract was drawn and reportedly sealed in the blood of the three participants. Immediately thereafter, a number of tersely coded telephone messages were relayed around the town and to Los Angeles, Las Vegas, Portland, Seattle, Honolulu, and Phoenix.

Meanwhile, less formal communications spread throughout the city via, mostly, word of mouth—with the result that "the silk suit brigade" disappeared suddenly from their usual haunts and became notably difficult to locate.

Speculation arose in various quarters that perhaps the underworld dragnet for Mack Bolan was falling apart.

At about six o'clock a "friend" at Harbor Precinct telephoned the DeMarco mansion with an urgent report to the effect that Captain Barney Gibson was quietly preparing a huge strike force to descend upon various quarters of Chinatown.

Several minutes later this same friend again called to breathlessly add to the earlier report. Gibson was also reportedly collecting warrants—secret warrants—for "a big sweep" early the following morning, this one directed against specific members of the Occidental community in and around Little Italy. It was further rumored that the warrants were being secretly coordinated with similar efforts in adjacent communities of the bay area.

At roughly twenty minutes past the hour of six, a physician was summoned to the DeMarco mansion to administer medication to a hypertensive old man.

As the doctor was departing, a man with an icy voice who identified himself as Mack Bolan was passed through to the DeMarco library via telephone. He talked to Tom the Broker Vericci and suggested that midnight could be the hour of doom—for everyone connected with Roman DeMarco. The caller gave special mention to a "Mr. King."

By seven o'clock all lights were lighted, inside and out, at the mansion on Russian Hill and jittery men prowled ceaselessly about the grounds and along the streets surrounding the property.

While, in the library, there was standing room only as the talk got down to the nitty-gritty business of personal survival in an uncertain world, and the hissing voice of *Don* DeMarco devoted itself to a series of cryptic telephone consultations with an unnamed "friend" who seemed entirely reluctant even to accept the calls.

Finally, at eight o'clock, DeMarco completed the

last of these telephone conversations and turned to his cadre with a relieved sigh.

"Okay," he reported tiredly. "It's set up. He'll meet with us in an hour. But we got to come alone. And we got to talk Wo Fan into coming with us."

At ten minutes past the hour of eight, a cautious acceptance from the Chinese community signalled a sure meet with Mr. King.

The hollow men, the stuffed men, had cast their vote to lean together ... to the bitter end.

From his eagle perch, Mack Bolan watched them depart—three big limousines moving slowly out of the drive and easing onto the streets of the city.

He scrutinized them closely, burning details into his scout's memory cells, and he watched until they turned down Lombard, "the crookedest street in the world."

Then he made the scramble to his battered, mud-streaked war chariot and picked up the procession as it crossed Taylor.

They made a stop and a pickup at the gates of Chinatown, and one of the vehicles remained there.

Bolan prudently made a swing around that plant and picked up the remaining two vehicles of the procession at the corner of Stockton and Sacramento.

They turned up Market. Bolan spotted them a light signal, then he swung out in casual pursuit.

The limousines went on all the way up Market to the Portola district, then started the climb toward Twin Peaks. Another vehicle dropped out there.

Bolan again ran a disengaging pattern and came onto the taillights of the target car halfway up the hill.

179

He was getting an idea, now, of where they were headed, and he relaxed a little. But not much. A pair of lights had kept swinging on him throughout the trip, dogging him all the way from way back on Russian Hill somewhere—or, at least, they seemed to be the same lights. He did not wish to get overly hung up on that rear vision—whatever might be back there, the target was ahead and this was where his primary concentration must be focused.

Twin Peaks is one of those "mustn't miss" tourist magnets of the San Francisco area, the geographic heart of the whole scenic wonderland that is San Francisco. From her overlooking peaks, which rise majestically above the other terrain like the proud thrust of a sleeping woman's breasts, the breathless visitor gets the entire bay area spread out below him and for a seemingly infinite distance, and it is especially spectacular at night time. In fact, the many observation-point lanes and pullovers once provided a heady lure to the lover's lane crowds, before the car-window bandits and rapists found the lure equally rewarding.

Bolan had been there many times, but neither as lover nor bandit, and tonight he was feeling a bit of tugging from both frames of consciousness. He was, he hoped, going to rob the mob ... and he was going to love doing it.

Not in any bloodthirsty sense, hell no. Bolan had long ago reached the point of gagging over blood offerings ... but, yeah, this was a damned important mission. Much more so than he had suspected just 24 short hours earlier. And he hoped, he hoped with an almost romantic fervor, that Twin Peaks was the appointed place for the meet. Up here, way up here where on a clear day the entire kingdom was spread out for inspection, would be the most ironically proper spot to meet the hollow men.

And, yeah, it was the place.

He saw the limousine pull into one of the little lanes which circle into a secluded observation park, and he killed his lights on the curve and dead-sticked it on in.

Something flickered in his rearview mirror as he rolled to his stop, but he could not be sure that it wasn't a reflection of distant city lights—and he for damn sure was not going to start chasing rear-guard phantoms at this point of the pursuit.

He snatched up the stuttergun and pulled a brief and silent recon to the rear, then he went on forward, sticking to the hillside and blending with the shadows until he was looking down on them.

The Mafia limousine was standing there with her horns to the safety rail, engine idling, parking lights on, all doors closed and the lights of town reflecting from raised windows.

A light standard rose up between the limousine and another car, a drab looking little foreign job, Japanese or something, and the lamp which was supposed to discourage smooching and robbing also seemed to be discouraging the lone occupant of the smaller vehicle.

Obviously, if they were to have any sort of meaningful discussions, they would have to take place in the limousine—and that would be crowded enough—or they would have to take place in the open air.

The guy was shy. Obviously he did not wish to leave his vehicle.

He had rolled down his window and was half-lying

across the seat in an effort to talk across to the limousine.

Bolan waited and watched.

Presently the doors of the limousine opened and the occupants slowly struggled to the outside.

Vericci was the first out. He had been driving. Then followed Ciprio and old man DeMarco and, finally, from the back seat, two gentlemen dudes of obvious Oriental backgrounds.

Bolan immediately recognized Wo Fan ... but the other guy ...

He whistled softly to himself and wondered. The commie? All the commissioners of California crime ... in one group?

Important, yeah. Maybe more important than Bolan could fully grasp.

The group straggled hesitantly toward the little import. Bolan automatically checked the safety switch on the burper and waited.

Come out, man, come out. Let me get a look at you before I rub you.

The guy didn't come out, but his head did, craning outward and upward beneath the overhanging lamp for a smiling welcome to his visiting dignitaries of despair.

Bolan stared at that face with a stunning recognition—and, for a moment, he tried to tell himself that he was not seeing what he thought he was seeing.

But then a lot of little things suddenly jogged together in that combat-hardened mind, and Bolan knew in a flash that indeed he was seeing "Mr. King" in the flesh ... and what a damned irony.

The name wasn't really King, of course. Almost as

big but not quite ... almost as respectable, but not quite.

Bolan felt his belly roll over and quiver, and he left those concealing shadows and moved silently across the paved surface for a close kill.

He did not want to miss this one. He did not want to miss this rotten son of a bitch ... this guy who was selling out not just his own people but maybe an entire nation in the bargain . . . this guy who killed and robbed and raped and starved and oppressed not just an occasional handful but thousands every day without ever experiencing the sight or smell or taste of blood in his delicate senses ... no, Bolan did not want to miss this guy.

DeMarco spotted the spectre of death first, and the old man made a move which could have passed as a clutching at a suddenly fibrillating heart, but it went on inside the coat and jerked rapidly back out again, and it was hauling hardware.

The others whirled at about that instant, and there was panic ... scraping feet and frightened grunts and diving hands ... even the guy inside the little car was fumbling with something on his dashboard ... and Bolan put everything he had ever been and ever hoped to be into that squeeze of the trigger.

He did not let off until the clip was dead, and all the hollow men had lost their stuffing, and were leaning together in a horizontal heap of carnal garbage.

He went over to the imported car, looked in, reached in, then withdrew and muttered, "Long live the king. The king is dead."

A voice behind him suggested, "Long live Able Team. Able Team is dead."

Bolan turned slowly, carefully, and stared into the tortured gaze of his old friend and flanker, Bill Phillips.

"That was you behind me," Bolan quietly decided.

"That was me, all the way."

"How'd you know?"

"You should know, Sarge. You taught me. I heard the cute stuff Gibson was letting leak. I put it together."

Bolan said, "Congratulations. You still intend to Wang Dang me?"

"It's my responsibility," the cop explained, regretfully.

Bolan nodded. He could understand that.

"Before you exercise that responsibility, Bill— remember, earlier today ... hell, was that just *today*?"

"Remember what?" Phillips prompted. He seemed to be begging, "Give me a reason not to, Sarge, just give me a reason I can live with."

But he didn't say it, and Bolan told him, "We were talking about the importance of certain missions. You know who these guys are, Bill?"

Phillips nodded his head. "Most of them."

"Look at the guy in the car."

"Nothing cute, Sarge. Just cool it."

"I'll cool it. Look in the car."

The tough Frisco Brushfire cop stepped carefully to the window, risked a quick look, then tossed an unbelieving glance at his captive and went in for a closer inspection.

He came out with his face all twisted in the anguish that only a black man can feel at certain times, and his gunhand dropped to his side, and he mumbled, "Okay. Goodbye Mack. Good luck."

Bolan replied, "Okay," and he turned and walked away from there.

Too bad, Bolan thought as he eased into the warwagon.

Yeah, too damned bad. Bolan knew. Or he thought he did. He thought he knew how tough it must get sometimes to simply *be* a black man.

Bill Phillips knew, for damned sure.

"Mr. King" would never know it again.

Long live the king. The king, God save his rotten soul, was dead.

EPILOGUE

Some wars, somehow, just didn't always seem worth winning.

Bolan finished his packing, and he told the China doll, "It's not that I'm in a rush to get away from you, Mary. It's just that I have this feeling. I've got to travel east, and damn quick."

"Personal business," she quietly suggested.

"Very personal business. Something very important—important like you, only different. Different, Mary."

"I guess we'll never meet again," she decided, sighing.

"Don't count on it." He gave her a solemn wink. "You, uh, square with Barney Gibson?"

She said, "I am. You made his day, soldier. More than that, I guess you made his life."

He slung the satchel over his back, went to the door, then turned about for a last long penetrating look at something very special that had briefly touched his life.

"Okay," he said.

Her face twisted as she replied, "Aren't you going out the window?"

He chuckled and told her, "I come in windows, lady, I don't go out them."

"Listen, tough guy," she said, her voice dropping to a harshly commanding tone, "you can climb in my window any old day ... or night. You come see me. You hear?"

He said, "I hear," and he gave her finally, fully, a total smile, and then he went out of there.

Something very important, more important than all the San Franciscos everywhere, was awaiting his attention in a distant eastern city.

No man could truly stand alone ... not forever. Only a fool would want to do so.

And if anything had happened to Johnny or Val ...

His stomach curled, and he commanded the thought to go away, even knowing that it would not.

If anything had happened to those two ... well, it would be a hellfire trail for sure, this time.

It would be a descent and a journey through the hell of all hells, and a lot of other dudes would share that fire with Mack Bolan.

Pittsfield, he quietly sent the word ahead, *I'm on my way.*

THE BEST IN PAPERBACKS FROM PINNACLE BOOKS!

ORDER NOW TO KEEP AHEAD!

To order, check the space next to the books you want, then mail your order, together with cash, check or money order, to: Pinnacle Books, Mail Order Dep't., Box 4347, Grand Central Station, New York, New York 10017.

Order No.	Title	Price
___P003	CATACLYSM, The Day The World Died	95¢
___P004	THE EXECUTIONER'S BATTLE MASK	95¢
___P005	BLOOD PATROL	95¢
___P006	THE GUNS OF TERRA 10	95¢
___P007	1989: POPULATION DOOMSDAY	95¢
___P008	MIAMI MASSACRE	95¢
___P009	KILLER PATROL	95¢
___P010	THE GODMAKERS	95¢
___P011	KILL QUICK OR DIE	95¢
___P012	CAST YOUR OWN SPELL	95¢
___P013	THE VEGAS TRAP	95¢
___P014	THE FEMINISTS	95¢
___P015	THE DEAD SEA SUBMARINE	95¢
___P016	STAY YOUNG WITH ASTROLOGY	95¢
___P017	THE EXECUTIONER: CONTINENTAL CONTRACT	95¢
___P018	TALKING TO THE SPIRITS	95¢
___P019	THE AVENGER TAPES	$1.25
___P020	TO CATCH A CROOKED GIRL	95¢
___P021	THE DEATH MERCHANT	95¢
___P022	THE GREAT STONE HEART	95¢
___P023	THE DEADLY SKY	95¢
___P024	THE DAY THE SUN FELL	$1.25
___P025	COME WATCH HIM DIE	95¢
___P026	SLATER'S PLANET	95¢
___P027	HOME IS WHERE THE QUICK IS: MOD SQUAD	95¢
___P028	EVERYTHING YOU NEED TO KNOW ABOUT ABORTION	$1.50
___P029	THE EXECUTIONER: ASSAULT ON SOHO	95¢
___P030	OPERATION RESCUE	$1.25
___P031	THE U.S. GOVERNMENT COOKBOOK	95¢

Order No.	Title	Price
___P032	TALES OF HORROR AND THE SUPERNATURAL, VOLUME ONE	95¢
___P033	FLIGHT OF HAWKS	95¢
___P034	PARADISE IS NOT ENOUGH	95¢
___P035	TERROR IN RIO	95¢
___P036	OTHER SIDE OF THE CLOCK	95¢
___P037	THE ESCAPE ARTIST	95¢
___P038	CREATED THE DESTROYER	95¢
___P039	THE EXECUTIONER, War Against The Mafia	95¢
___P040	THE EXECUTIONER'S DEATH SQUAD	95¢
___P041	LOVE SONG	$1.25
___P042	THE NEW COOK'S COOKBOOK	$1.25
___P043	THE ALIEN EARTH	95¢
___P044	THE EXECUTIONER: NIGHTMARE IN NEW YORK	95¢
___P046	THE RECTOR	95¢
___P047	LOVE, AMERICAN STYLE, 1	95¢
___P048	THE SPRINGING OF GEORGE BLAKE	$1.50
___P049	THE BELLS OF WIDOW'S BAY	95¢
___P050	IMPERIAL TRAGEDY	$1.95
___P051	THE EXECUTIONER: CHICAGO WIPEOUT	95¢
___P052	THE GOLDEN OYSTER	95¢
___P053	DAUGHTER OF HENRY VIII	95¢
___P054	TALES FROM THE UNKNOWN	95¢
___P055	CIVIL WAR II	95¢
___P056	FOURTH STREET EAST	$1.25
___P057	HOW TO MARRY A MARRIED MAN	95¢
___P058	THE GROUPSEX SCENE	$1.25
___P059	THE EXECUTIONER: VEGAS VENDETTA	95¢
___P060	THE VALIANT SAILORS	95¢
___P061	SABERLEGS	95¢
___P062	FIRST CONTACT	95¢
___P063	TIMES AND PLACES	$1.25
___P064	THE CLASH OF DISTANT THUNDER	95¢
___P065	CALLEY: SOLDIER OR KILLER	95¢
___P066	NAKED, AS AN AUTHOR	95¢
___P067	GUNS FOR GENERAL LI	95¢
___P068	PURR, BABY, PURR	$1.25
___P069	THE PENTAGON	$1.95

Order No.	Title	Price
___P070	BRAVE CAPTAINS	95¢
___P071	CONGO WAR CRY	95¢
___P072	THE DESTROYER: DEATH CHECK	95¢
___P073	101 BEST GROWTH STOCKS FOR 1972	$1.25
___P074	DUELING OAKS	95¢
___P075	CHARTING THE CANDIDATES	$1.25
___P076	THE EXECUTIONER: CARIBBEAN KILL	95¢
___P078	THE DESTROYER: CHINESE PUZZLE	95¢
___P079	DIAMOND RIVER	95¢
___P080	LEAP IN THE DARK	95¢
___P081	LOVE, AMERICAN STYLE, 2	95¢
___P083	HAZARD'S COMMAND	95¢
___P084	KEEPERS OF DEATH	95¢
___P085	DEATH MERCHANT: OPERATION OVERKILL	95¢
___P086	WHERE SHADOWS LIE	95¢
___P088	RELAXERCISES	$1.25
___P090	BURN AFTER READING	95¢
___P091	DOWN THE TUBE	$1.25
___P092	HOW TO "MAKE IT" 365 DAYS A YEAR	$1.25
___P093	THE CANARIS CONSPIRACY	$1.25
___P094	HANNIE CAULDER	95¢
___P095	THE EXECUTIONER: CALIFORNIA HIT	95¢
___P096	GOLD WAGON	95¢
___P097	AFGHAN ASSAULT	95¢
___P098	EXECUTIVE YOGA	$1.25
___P105	BLUE MARSH	95¢

Pinnacle Books, Box 4347, Grand Central Station, New York, New York 10017

Gentlemen:

Please send me the books I have marked. I enclose_____ as payment in full. (Sorry, no CODs.)

Name_____

Address_____

City_____State_____Zip_____